MALAFORMED REALITIES

VOLUME FIVE

THOMAS M. MALAFARINA

HELLBENDER
BOOKS

an imprint of Sunbury Press, Inc.
Mechanicsburg, PA USA

an imprint of Sunbury Press, Inc.
Mechanicsburg, PA USA

For information about special discounts for bulk purchases, please contact Sunbury Press Orders Dept. at (855) 338-8359 or orders@sunburypress.com.

To request one of our authors for speaking engagements or book signings, please contact Sunbury Press Publicity Dept. at publicity@sunburypress.com.

FIRST HELLBENDER BOOKS EDITION: August 2021

Set in Adobe Garamond | Interior design by Crystal Devine | Cover design by Lawrence Knorr | Edited by Lawrence Knorr.

Publisher's Cataloging-in-Publication Data
Names: Malafarina, Thomas M., author.
Title: Malaformed realities / Thomas M. Malafarina.
Description: First trade paperback edition. | Mechanicsburg, PA : Hellbender Books, 2021.
Summary: Thomas Malafarina strikes again with 31 spine-tingling tales of horror.
Identifiers: ISBN 978-1-62006-882-3 (softcover).
Subjects: FICTION / Horror | FICTION / Short Stories (single author).

Product of the United States of America
0 1 1 2 3 5 8 13 21 34 55

Continue the Enlightenment!

*For my incredible wife, JoAnne.
I have dedicated every book I've written
to you yet it hardly seems enough And
even though you prefer not to have me
sing your praises or shower you with
affection, I can neither help myself
or stop, as you deserve it all and more.*

CONTENTS

Introduction . . . 1

Don't Stare, Don't Point . . . 3

Jumper . . .9

The Clan . . . 14

Two Graves . . . 18

Let Me Out . . . 22

Welcome Home Cindy . . . 31

White Rooms . . . 35

Chains Of Love . . . 42

Insanity . . . 48

Dead Pumpkins . . . 57

He Knows When You're Awake . . . 60

The Bewilderment of Harry Easton . . . 66

The Golden Ankh . . . 73

Legs . . . 79

Relax . . . 85

Image Is Everything . . . 90

Worms . . . 96

Bait and Switch . . . 102

The Horton Mountain Ghost . . . 107

People Are Strange . . . 110

Jacob's Tree . . . 116

More Than a Feeling . . . 120

Revolting Candy Company . . . 124

Harvest Home . . . 137

Sub Sandwiches . . . 141

Nightmare Shadows . . . 145

Faces In a Crowd . . . 151

Haerid's Deal . . . 156

What Is a Man? . . . 164

Parallelism . . . 174

INTRODUCTION

Here we are with the fifth edition of Malaformed Realities. Wow. Then again, my short stories have to go somewhere with over one hundred and fifty written to date. So, why not in a series where someone can come and get a sampling of my works ranging from pure horror to sci-fi horror to fantasy horror. Notice a common theme here? Yep, horror.

Like the four previous collections in the series, *Malaformed Realities Volume 5* is chocked full of all sorts of goodies. From the strange to the frightening to the mysterious to the downright disgusting, Malaformed Realities has it all. So please sit back, turn the lights down low and enjoy the many twisted tales you'll find in *Malaformed Realities Volume 5*.

THOMAS M. MALAFARINA
2021

DON'T STARE, DON'T POINT

"It's quite stressful knowing that every time you walk out the door,
someone is going to be giving you a very good look up and down,
judging everything you wear."
—EMMA WATSON

"I'm not the judge. You know, God didn't tell me to go around
judging everybody."
—JOEL OSTEEN

"Justin Thurston Williamson, you stop that this minute. How
many times do I have to tell you? It's impolite to stare and downright
rude to point! You wouldn't like it if people did that to you."

That's what Justin Williamson's mother often told him back when
he was a kid. However, now that he was a grown man of almost fifty, it
seemed not only had he not learned his mother's lessons, but his wife
Britney had taken over where his mother had left off.

"Dammit, Justin! How many times have I told you not to gawk at
people and, for the love of God, don't stand there pointing at them? It's
embarrassing. I don't care how odd, strange, weird, or freaky they may
seem; you simply don't have the right to point them out and stare at
them. I'm sure you wouldn't like it if someone stood around pointing
and gaping like that at you."

"Yes, Mot . . . I mean, yes, dear," he replied, realizing he had almost said, "Yes, Mother." Whoa! That wouldn't have been a good thing by any stretch of the imagination. Because not only was his wife a lot like his long-dead mother but there were times when Justin felt as if she was his mother, reincarnated. He didn't want to begin to think about what such a concept might say about him. He decided it was probably better to keep those sorts of ideas out of his head.

"But seriously, Britt, did you see the size of that woman? She was massive. She was huge! No, she was huger than huge! She was humongous!" He started to raise his finger to point at the oversized woman again.

His wife slapped his hand down, "Justin Thurston Williamson! Don't you dare point your finger at that poor, disabled woman! She can't help it if she's disabled and has to ride around the store on that electric cart."

"Lard cart, you mean."

"Stop that! It's not funny to make a mockery of someone's disability."

"Disability? Look at the way her enormous butt hangs over both sides of the seat of that cart. It looks like two saddlebags on the back of a Harley, fat boy. It's a wonder the seat doesn't get sucked up inside her sphincter and never seen again. Look, Britt, the only disability that particular woman has is that the hole in her mouth is bigger than the one in her butt. Input exceeds output, simple math."

"But maybe she has some leg or back trouble that causes her not to be able to walk or exercise. If that's the case, she can't help but gain weight, and you shouldn't assume that she's lazy."

"It's likely a case of which came first, the chicken or the egg. Did that lady become fat because she overeats and can't exercise, or is it that she can't exercise because she overeats and is fat?"

"We don't know the answer to that. We don't know anything about the poor woman. Therefore, we have no right to judge. And we especially have no right to point and stare."

"But take a look at her husband or boyfriend or whatever the heck he is standing over there. He's skinny as a rail. What's his deal? And tell me, why is it that these enormously fat chicks always have some scrawny little man following them around like a puppy? These guys have got to be enablers, allowing those freaks to get so fat by doing everything for them. Maybe these guys are just chubby chasers and figure as long as they keep their women huge, no one else will bother with them."

"That's a terrible thing to say," Brittney scolded, looking down at herself, "I'm not exactly skin and bones, you know. I'm sure you wouldn't want people talking about me that way."

"Look, Britt. We all could stand to drop a few pounds, myself included, but these broads could stand to drop a few people, for God's sake."

He pointed at another large woman riding one of the handicapped scooters through the store. "Look at that bovine over there. You could put her in a printed tent dress and have an image of her on a banner for a sideshow, billing her as the incredible fat woman."

"I think you'd better stop this sort of talk right now, Justin. It's rude, inconsiderate, and does nothing to make you look good in anyone's eyes."

Then he pointed off in another direction, "And look at that mutant over there. He's got more tattoos and body piercings than anyone I've ever seen. He could be the star of a sideshow and billed as "The Human Pin Cushion" or "The Illustrated Man." Take a minute to look around you, Britt; the world has become an admission-free freak show, with a new oddity around every corner. No wonder you seldom see freak shows in circuses anymore. How could they possibly compete with what we see shopping here every day? So how can I help but point and stare?"

"You know Justin, someday this is all going to backfire on you, and this staring, pointing, and commenting is going to get you into big trouble."

"Trouble? Seriously? What sort of trouble could it possibly cause? It's a free country, and if some weirdo wants to parade around the same streets with normal people, then they should expect to get stared at."

"I don't know what sort of trouble could occur, but I'm telling you, Justin, no good can come of your persistent and annoying behavior."

"I think you're taking all of this a bit too seriously, Britt. It's not that big of a deal, and it's not like I do it all the time. Whoa, heads up, incoming, look over there!" He pointed toward the entrance to the store, "Now that's a real freak if I ever saw one."

"Oh my God, Justin. How can you be so insensitive? You should pity that man, not ridicule him."

"What man? Don't you mean men, as in more than one?"

Justin had been pointing at what Brittney thought at first to be a hunched-back man. But after closer examination, she realized what she saw was two men. One was normal-sized and hunched over. There was another smaller man who appeared to be attached to the front of the larger man.

"Siamese twins! Bingo! Score!" Justin shouted much louder than he should have, "Now, don't that just beat all? This store really must be a freak magnet. I mean, it's like flypaper for mutants."

"Oh, Justin! You're despicable! I've had enough of your comments. I'm leaving. You can stay here pointing and staring to your heart's content."

Brittney reached into her purse and withdrew her car keys.

"But you drove me here. How in the hell am I supposed to get home?"

"That's your problem, Justin. Maybe if you go out front in the parking lot and point at a taxicab, one will stop for you. I don't care what you do, Justin. I've had enough of you and your rude behavior for one day."

Brittany turned and walked out of the store, leaving her husband standing behind her, baffled, mouth agape.

He mumbled to himself, "I wonder what the hell's gotten into her. I mean, seriously. You make a few comments, point out a few physical flaws, and suddenly you're a bad guy? Oh well, I suppose there's nothing I can do about it now. I might as well get my shopping out of the way. Then I guess I'll call for a cab or something."

Justin turned to walk further into the store and suddenly stopped in his tracks. A crowd of strange-looking people blocked his path.

There had to be at least ten of them, all standing and silently staring at him. Every single one of them fit right into the category of what Justin considered to be freaks. There was a man on crutches with one leg, the empty pant leg pinned up to keep it from flapping uselessly, and a woman in a motorized wheelchair whose legs were tiny and shriveled from atrophy under her small pants. He saw the fat woman on the handicapped cart and her skinny partner. The tattooed character he thought of as the illustrated man was there as well. And at the front of the crowd stood the Siamese twins he had most recently noticed.

"Um, ah. Is there something I can do for you?" Justin asked, suddenly feeling the hairs on the back of his neck stand on end.

After several awkward moments, the tattooed man said, "You pointed at us. We saw you." Then as one, the crowd took a single step forward, feet and crutches simultaneously slapping the floor and sounding like an army on the march.

"You stared at us too," the one-legged man snarled. The crowd took another step closer.

"And you laughed at us," the fat woman said as they came even closer.

"You called us freaks," the larger Siamese twin said, followed by another step closer.

"Yeah, freaks," his smaller, conjoined brother agreed in a much higher pitch voice as they all took yet another step closer.

Justin got a good look at just how twisted and deformed the conjoined twins were. The smaller one only had a small right arm and part of a right leg. He appeared to be growing out from his brother's chest, which in essence, he was.

The larger brother said, "I wonder how you'd feel if everywhere you went, people stared and pointed at you?"

"And laughed at you and called you a freak," Some unidentified voice in the crowd shouted.

The look of the twins had so enthralled Justin; he hadn't realized the gang of oddities had somehow surrounded him.

The larger of the conjoined twins said, "But you'll know exactly how it feels very soon." That was when they all fell upon him.

///

"Justin. I'm going to the store," Brittney called. "Are you sure you don't want to come along? We have to try to get you out of the house more. I know you don't like going out in public much anymore, but maybe just this one time? It might be good for you."

She hesitated for a moment then called, "Very well; maybe next time. I won't be very long. See you soon." She was doing her best to cope with the guilt she still felt at having gotten so angry that day several months earlier when she left Justin alone in the store.

Justin didn't reply. He seldom did anymore, not since that day. He used his two twisted arms to try to struggle and lift himself into a sitting position. As difficult as this was, it had become a lot easier now that his heavy, useless, crushed legs had to be amputated. It was unbelievable how much their dead weight had slowed him down. He looked around his bedroom through his one good eye. It was the one on the side of his face that they hadn't smashed in the attack. He was also starting to see hair finally growing in random patches between the ruined areas of his pink, tender scalp. That was where the mob had torn his hair out by the roots.

He hoped someday he'd be ready to go out in public again, but he had no idea when that might be, if it ever would be at all. He knew he needed to get out and couldn't spend the rest of his life cooped up in his house. Justin knew, however, that he couldn't accept the thought that people might be staring and pointing at him.

JUMPER

"Never contend with a man who has nothing to lose."
—BALTASAR GRACIÁN

The man sat uncomfortably on the narrow ledge, his back pressed tight against the brick wall behind him. He could feel the rough surface of the wall imprinting itself into the sweating flesh of his back. The cold of the concrete ledge seeped into his firmly flattened palms. He could see the flashing lights of several police patrol cars, fire trucks, ambulances, news vans, and rescue vehicles many stories far below. Just looking down at them gave him a feeling of vertigo that was almost overwhelming.

Under other circumstances, the entire event might have proven fascinating, perhaps even exciting. It probably felt that way to the crowd of lookie-loos who stood behind police lines. Although their faces were too far away to see, Jerome could occasionally hear laughter coming from the group. Several people even began shouting, "Jump!" until the police officers ordered them to silence.

Yes, Jerome could see how such a spectacle might provide unexpected entertainment for people caught up in their everyday rat race. He never entirely understood, however, how someone could get pleasure from another person's tragedy. He wondered what they would think when he finally allowed himself to slide gently off the ledge and fall more than a dozen stories to the hard concrete below. Would they applaud? Would they ooh and ahh like a group of people watching fireworks? Or would they suddenly realize the horror of what they had not only allowed to happen but had helped to encourage? He wondered, but he didn't care. Caring was not a luxury for someone with nothing to lose.

Then he speculated as to what Theresa would think when she heard about it on the evening news. There were plenty of news vans on the street below and even several news helicopters circling the building, although they had to keep their distance. Jerome couldn't make out the pilots' faces or the men behind the video cameras in the copters. He supposed they had zoom lenses and could see him quite well, however.

Would his wife feel sad when she learned he had jumped to his death? Would she watch the video of his final moments of life? Or would she even care? He supposed that no longer mattered either. She wasn't his Teresa anymore. Soon he'd be leaving all of his sorrow and heartbreak behind, and it would all be over for him.

"So, are you really going to do this?" A voice suddenly said from his right. Jerome was so startled he almost fell from the ledge. Although this might have been fine, he didn't want his death to be an accident. He needed to make sure his death plunge was spectacular and that everyone knew a broken-hearted man killed himself after being jilted by the love of his life.

"Who, who the hell are you?" Jerome said as he gulped to try to remove his heart from his throat. A stranger was sitting on the ledge not more than three feet away from him. He looked behind the man and saw the open window, the one which the stranger must have used to come out on the ledge, the same window Jerome had used before scooting down out of the reach of any would-be heroes. The man wore a pair of plain blue jeans, a tee-shirt, and running shoes. He appeared to be a bit older than Jerome.

"Are you a cop?" Jerome asked after not getting a response to his first inquiry.

"No. Nope. I'm no cop. I'm no firefighter or rescue worker, or even a shrink. I'm just some guy who wants to talk you out of making the worse mistake of your life."

"Mistake? I'm not making a mistake. Look, Buddy."

"Charley. My name's Charley."

"Fine. Look, Charley. I know what I'm doing. I have to do this. My wife, Teresa, left me for another man. I've tried to cope with it, but the pain is just too much for me. For a while, I was angry, so angry I wanted to kill her and her new lover."

Charley smiled, shrugged his shoulders, and said, "Women: can't live with 'em. Can't kill 'em."

"Uh. Yeah. Very funny. Forgive me all to hell for not breaking out in fits of laughter."

"Sorry, man. I didn't mean to make light of the situation. It's just I know where you're coming from, and I understand."

"What does that mean? How can you possibly understand?"

"I understand because I was sitting exactly where you were sitting about three years ago, and I was all set to take the big leap just like you're planning to do."

"You, you were? Why? What happened to you, Charley?"

"Pretty much the same situation you're going through, Jerome. May I call you Jerome?"

"Yeah, sure. But hey, how do you know my name?"

"That's not important, Jerome, but this is. My girl Penny left me for a rich man. I was devastated. I knew there was no way in hell I could compete with someone like that. I was a general laborer in a local factory. I made decent money but not the sort of cash that guy had."

"So, you came up here, ready to jump to your death because you felt your life was over and you had nothing to lose, just like me."

"Yeah. Something like that."

"And allow me to take a wild guess at what happened, someone stuck their head out that window, some cop or shrink, and convinced you that your life wasn't over. Then you crawled back to the window and allowed the savior to help you in. And now, after several years of counseling, you realized the error of your ways, and you've found your purpose in life. And that purpose happens to be helping to keep poor slobs like me from splatting themselves on the sidewalk. Yadda, yadda, yadda. Right?"

"No. Well, not exactly. That's not quite how things turned out."

"What do you mean?"

"Well, Jerome. There are a couple of things you might not have taken into account when you planned this freefall. That is if you planned it at all. Sometimes these are just spur-of-the-moment sorts of things. Anyway, do you realize, Jerome, that in many if not most religions, they teach that suicide is a one-way ticket to Hell?"

"Of course, I do. I haven't been spending my life living under a rock. Everyone's heard that. But you know Charley, I've never been a big believer in religion, and right now, thoughts of Heaven or Hell are so far off my radar that there's little point in us having this conversation."

"Au contraire, mon frère. I beg to differ. Hell is something you need to think about before you take the plunge."

"Nonsense," Jerome insisted.

"Fine, well, another thing to consider is you could accidentally land on someone down there and kill them in the process. That would make this murder/suicide. Not a very good end, cosmically speaking."

"That's not my concern; if somebody gets in my way, then too bad for him."

"Or think about this. You might not die right away. Maybe you'll fatally injure yourself, but it might take minutes or hours for you to die, in which case you'll be in extreme agony for quite a while."

"No way. I'm sure I die instantly. And I don't believe I'll go to Hell either."

"Ok. So maybe you won't go to Hell. Maybe instead, you'll go nowhere. Maybe your spirit will linger between life and death, a lost soul forced to roam around aimlessly for eternity. Did you ever think about that one, Jerome?"

"Don't you see Charley? It doesn't matter what happens to me. It's all over for me now, and nothing else matters."

Then the stranger reached out and placed his hand on top of Jerome's hand. Suddenly Jerome was sliding off the ledge and could see the ground below coming up to meet him in slow motion. He could hear screams and gasps from the crowd as he plunged to his certain death. Then with a slam, his body hit the concrete, and agony shot through every inch of him as Jerome lay staring out at the oncoming feet of rescue workers. He was still alive but in pain, incredible pain the likes of which he had never experienced in his entire life. He hadn't died!

Suddenly he opened his eyes and found himself dangerously close to the edge of the ledge. Several people in the crowd below were screaming at him to get back. His head felt strange, his thoughts jumbled. He felt dizzy. Slowly he pressed himself back against the brick of the building. What had just happened? He wasn't dead. He was still on the ledge.

"Hey, buddy," a voice called from his right. Jerome slowly turned and saw a rescue worker leaning out of the open window. "Look, Pal. I don't know what's eating at you but believe me, it's not worth killing yourself over. Why don't you slide over here and let me bring you inside?"

The man's voice was calm and reassuring. Before Jerome realized what was happening, he slid along the ledge, working his way over to the window. Within a few minutes, strong hands grabbed him and pulled him safely inside. He could hear a mixture of cheers and boos coming from the onlookers far below.

"It's going to be ok now," the rescue worker said. "You're going to be all right now."

"But where's that other guy?"

"What other guy?" The rescue worker asked.

"That guy Charley who was sitting next to me."

"Sorry, Pal. There was nobody out there with you. It must have been the stress of everything playing mind tricks on you. The last guy on that ledge took a header about three years ago. It was a mess. The poor slob hit the ground and broke almost every bone in his body. And the worst part was he didn't die right away. He lay there for several minutes in agony before he finally clocked out. Hey! Come to think about it; I believe his name was Charley."

THE CLAN

The silver moon shone brightly in the Eastern sky, its effervescent glow casting a blanket of luminescence over the tops of the canopy of trees. The density of the overhanging foliage prevented all but the slightest elements of moon glow from penetrating down to the pitch-black forest floor below, where a unique and sacred ceremony was supposed to occur. However, an unexpected and heated argument had broken out among the participants.

"This must end, and it must end now," Serr-Bann demanded from his shadowed side of the sacred circle.

His protests were immediately cut short by the deep, bellowing voice of the clan leader Sharr-Tann, "What you suggest is blasphemous Serr-Bann. It is the new moon of this sector, and as always, we must offer a sacrifice."

On a blanket a distance away from the sacred circle, an infant girl lay wrapped tightly in a blanket. She slept quietly, unaware of the argument taking place just several feet from where she lay.

"You are wrong, Sharr-Tann. Human sacrifice was the way of the old ones. It was wrong then, and it's wrong now. It's a practice whose time has passed and one which must end now."

Sharr-Tann bellowed with savage anger, his voice seeming to tear a hole in the fabric of darkness, "Hold your heathen tongue, Serr-Bann! How dare you say such a thing during the sacred ceremony and at this holiest of places? We stand here in the 'Clearing of the Giving,' the place of sacrifice. The gods of the trees and forest hear every word we say. Do you wish to bring their wrath down upon us? Do you wish for us to starve to death because of their anger?"

"Gods? What Gods Sharr-Tann? I see no gods. There are no gods here in the forest! There are no gods anywhere! We are all there is! Whether we live or die is not the will of some imaginary deity, it is dependent upon our survival abilities."

A series of gasps erupted from the darkness as the other clan members reacted in stunned disbelief, unable to comprehend how Serr-Bann could say such a thing. And to do so in the 'Clearing of the Giving' no less was unprecedented.

"Have you lost your mind, Serr-Bann? Do you want the gods to strike us all dead because of your sacrilegious comments? As the leader and high priest of this clan, I order you to stop your sinful talk immediately, or I swear by the great god Woo-Denn, I will tear your beating heart from your chest and sacrifice your corpse along with that of the child."

"No, you will not silence me! For far too many years, I've watched you take the lives of so many innocents in the name of your false gods, Sharr-Tann. So may young ones murdered by your hand. I can stand by no longer. I'm sorry, Sharr-Tann, but this must stop, and as such, I have no choice but to offer myself to the challenge."

Again, in the darkness, the other clan members gasped in disbelief. To offer the challenge was to demand a battle to the death. But for one to offer such a challenge to the great Sharr-Tann, leader and high priest was akin to suicide. He was the largest, the strongest, and the deadliest member of the clan. If that were not enough, he had the power of the gods of the forest behind him. No sane clan member would ever issue such an outlandish challenge. Although Serr-Bann was almost as big as Sharr-Tann and was well suited for the battle, he didn't have the fighting experience, nor did he wield the mysterious power of the forest gods.

"What? Do you dare offer me the sacred challenge? Are you mad, Serr-Bann? I will tear you to pieces, and the gods will curse your descendants for thousands of sectors to come."

"No, Sharr-Tann. You may try, but you will not win this challenge."

The other clan members shuffled backward in the darkness, creating a circular clearing for what they knew would be a fight to the death. None of them wanted any part of such a conflict. They knew and respected both opponents for their strength and cunning but understood that clan law prevented them from intervening regardless of their loyalties.

The two opponents approached each other in the center circle, stalking the other in the almost complete darkness, their eyes burning like glowing embers in the minimal moonlight. Their hair stood high on the backs of their necks in anticipation of the fight. The air had become completely silent, so much so that Serr-Bann could hear the gentle breathing of the infant in the distance. He knew he was the child's only hope for survival. He tensed every muscle in his body, and before he had a chance to change his mind, he sprung at Sharr-Tann.

The death battle, which followed, would be repeated in tribal tales for decades to follow. What seemed like gallons of gore turned the soil into mud. After what seemed like an hour, all the bloody savagery was over, and only one survived, Serr-Bann. The great and feared Sharr-Tann was dead.

With exhausted breath, Serr-Bann proclaimed, "You know the law. I'm now the leader of this clan. Do any of you want to challenge me?" There was only silence.

"Very well. Who among you was responsible for bringing the child here to be sacrificed?" He demanded.

After several moments of silence, a lone voice spoke up timidly, "It was I, Serr-Bann. I, Jarr-Haan, brought the babe on the orders of Sharr-Tann."

"Fear not, Jarr-Haan. You were following the laws of the clan, but now those laws have ended with the life of Sharr-Tann. Now my laws prevail. You must return this child, unharmed to his family. Do so with the same stealth you used to take her; else, you might be captured and killed in the process. Do you understand?"

"I understand great Serr-Bann." The clansman walked over to the baby and carefully lifted the bundle in his massive, fang-filled jaws. He turned and nodded to the darkness, which held the rest of his pack, and padded away on his four enormous, clawed paws into the forest to return the human child to its family.

"The day of human sacrifice is over. The 'Clearing of the Giving' is no more. Neither are the false gods of the trees and forest. We are entering a new era, a time when we can learn to become gentle and civilized like humanity."

TWO GRAVES

Before you embark on a journey of revenge, dig two graves.
—CONFUCIUS

Sweat dripped from the brow of the frail man laboring in the oppressive heat of the dark August night. Shovelful by shovelful, he slowly removed dirt from the ever-expanding hole. His muscles had stopped screaming with agony an hour earlier, and now a dull ache seemed to course throughout his exhausted body. Such intense manual labor was foreign to him. He was an accountant, for God's sake, a numbers man.

He wondered why it was the ground couldn't be soft, rich farm soil. Why did it have to be thick, unforgiving clay? Not that it mattered in the scheme of things. Whether he dropped dead of exhaustion from digging or waited for the maniac to shoot him, either way, he was going to end up buried in this hole. He attempted to wipe the sweat away with an arm caked with grime.

"Keep digging, Kensington," the gruff voice commanded. That voice belonged to Vito Montenegro, head of the local crime syndicate and Willard Kensington's former boss. Standing silently next to him was Gomo, his henchman and chief executioner. Willard didn't know Gomo's real name. Still, the silent, ape-like giant was legendary for both the number of people he had murdered on Montenegro's orders as well as those poor individuals who he had tortured for hours before killing them. Willard supposed he was lucky to have avoided any such festival of pain with the maniac and that Montenegro had decided to shoot him outright. That is if one could consider getting shot lucky.

With a trembling voice, Willard begged, "Please, Mr. Montenegro, rethink what you're doing here. I've told you how sorry I was for stealing money from you and I returned every cent with interest, didn't I? That has to be worth something. Can't you consider sparing me? I promise I'll leave the state if you want. Hell, I'll leave the country if that'll make you happy, and I swear, and you'll never have to see me again. Just please let me live, I beg you."

"But Kensington, after tonight, not only will you be leaving the country, but you'll be leaving the planet. And the only way I'll ever have to see you again is if I choose to dig up your rotting corpse. I'm sorry, Kensington, but I can't let such a slight against me go unpunished. You know that about me. Now I strongly suggest you get back to work."

"But please, hear me out. Killing me isn't the answer, Mr. Montenegro. Revenge is never the answer. Didn't you ever hear the proverb from the great philosopher Confucius? He said, 'Before you embark on a journey of revenge, dig two graves.'"

"No, I haven't heard it. Nor do I care, Kensington. Besides, what the hell is that supposed to mean anyway?"

Thinking he might yet have a chance to save his skin if he could only convince Montenegro, Willard said, "It means, in committing the act of murder based on vengeance, you'll hurt yourself as much as your victim. Understand what he was saying? One of the two graves is for your victim, and the other is for yourself."

"So, you're trying to tell me that if I have Gomo here kill you, then either he or I will also die?"

"No, that's not it. See, you won't die as you might think of it, but a part of you will die inside. If you kill enough people, which you probably have over the years, then someday you'll be deader inside than you are alive."

Montenegro thought about this for a moment, and then he looked around the area, pointed, and said, "See that place over there underneath the oak tree Kensington; the place where the ground is slightly rounded?"

"Um, yes," Willard said, looking over at the spot, instinctively understanding exactly where the conversation was about to head.

"And that spot over there?" Montenegro said, "And those three spots over there? Those and many others around here contain bodies. Those people like yourself thought they were so smart. They also tried to make a fool out of me. They are dead, yet here I am, still alive. If I'm dead inside, how am I still standing here speaking with you? You see, Kensington, I do not need a second grave. I only need the one you're digging, and that my friend is for you."

"But don't you realize? Each time you kill someone, your soul dies a little more. Don't you ever worry that at some point down the road, you'll have to answer for that? What exactly do you think will happen to you and Gomo when you reach that point? Don't you ever worry about that? For all you know, killing me tonight might be the act that finally pushes your dying soul beyond the brink."

Willard had no idea what he was saying or if any of it made sense whatsoever. He was just rambling. He was just saying anything and everything he could think of to try to stay alive, even if just for a few minutes longer.

"Stop talking, Kensington, and keep digging, or I'll have Gomo here shoot you now."

Willard went silent and resumed his labor. After another hour of uninterrupted digging, Montenegro said, "Alright, Kensington. That should be deep enough. Come up out of there."

The man crawled out of the hole, and Gomo grabbed him by the arm, forcing Willard to his knees at the base of the shallow grave. Willard felt the cold barrel of Gomo's gun against the back of the head, and he knew in just seconds they'd shoot him and shove his body into the grave. Willard closed his eyes, prayed silently to himself as he awaited his fate.

After a few seconds, he heard what sounded like shuffling all around him. He kept his eyes tightly shut, waiting for the gunshot. He heard Gomo grunt, felt the barrel of the gun pull away from his head.

Montenegro shouted, "What the hell?"

Then Willard heard the gun blast, but instead of dying, he realized he was still kneeling next to the grave. Several more gun blasts followed, then a clicking sound indicating the gun was empty. There was a scuffling behind him, followed by the sound of screams of agony. Willard slowly turned his head and opened his eyes to see what was happening and what he saw shocked and horrified to the point of near-paralysis.

All around him, the places Montenegro had pointed out as burial sites for his victims had dirt piled near them, looking as if someone had dug up the corpses. As revolting as that idea may have been, what had happened was far worse. His heart practically froze in his chest when he saw. A dozen or more rotting corpses had dug their way out of their graves and surrounded Montenegro and Gomo. Each horrifying creature was grabbing and clawing at the pair of thugs, tearing and ripping at their flesh and clothing. Gomo had pumped shot after shot into the hell-spawned things, yet they kept coming. Within a few minutes, which seemed like an eternity, the two criminals had fallen to the ground where the creatures dropped on them and began tearing them to pieces.

When they finished, the monsters stood, then turned to the still kneeling Willard Kensington, who was now weeping uncontrollably. He was sure they were going to fall on him next. However, one creature at the front of the pack first pointed to the ravaged remains of the gangsters. Then it pointed to the hole Willard had dug and nodded. Too terrified to do anything else, Willard stared mouth agape, mindlessly nodding back at the creatures. Next, one by one, the undead monsters slowly began shuffling back to their respective graves, where they laid down and pulled the dirt in on top of themselves.

Willard stood and looked and the carnage, which was all that remained of Gomo and Montenegro. Then he looked down at the hole they had forced him to dig for himself. With revulsion churning deep in the pit of his stomach, Willard began to drag the remains of his would-be assassins over, dropping them piece by piece into the grave.

Later, when he had covered the bodies and filled in the grave, Willard looked down at the fresh mound of earth and said, "Well, I suppose you were right, Mr. Montenegro. It looks like one grave was enough."

LET ME OUT

"The battleline between good and evil runs through
the heart of every man"
—ALEKSANDR SOLZHENITSYN

"It is a man's own mind, not his enemy or foe,
that lures him to evil ways"
—BUDDHA

"Life is neither good nor evil, but only a place
for good and evil"
—MARCUS AURELIUS

"Erickson? Can I see you in my office? Immediately" The old man said sternly over the phone. Paul Erickson knew what this meant. It meant what it always meant. Old man Dick Barker, his boss, was unhappy with something Paul had said or done. That told Paul it was time for one of Barker's boring lectures, one of those where the man droned on for what seemed like hours.

Paul dreaded these endless sermons. The worst thing about them wasn't simply that Barker was in love with the sound of his miserable voice. That would have been bad enough. The real problem was that the man thought he was doing good and mentoring his subordinates with his pontifications. He honestly believed he was making his workers better employees when he was boring them to death and making them crazy.

Paul often thought, "Dick Barker is a perfect name for you, old man. For starters, you are a dick, and you can't stop yourself from barking."

But he would never say this aloud; he just didn't need the aggravation. He had responsibilities; he had his family depending upon him. Yes, with his skills and education, he could probably find another job in a week, but the truth was it was easier to put up with Barker than to start over somewhere else. So, Paul would always sit quietly like a good little soldier, pretending to be listening to every word his glorious mentor chose to expel from that flatulent hole in his face.

Dick Barker was hands down the king of cliches and the baron of office buzzwords. One of the expressions Barker used far too often and one which drove Paul insane was, "Perception is reality."

He would say, "Paul, my boy, you have to realize in this world, perception is reality. If you want to succeed in this or any other company, you have to project an image of someone worthy of succeeding." Then he would drone on and on about the importance of physical appearance, punctuality, work ethic, saying the right thing, sense of urgency, and on and on and on.

It wasn't that Paul felt the recommendations were wrong or outdated; he agreed with Barker's ideas. The problem was he knew all of this already. Paul had known it for twenty years. He had started working for Barker right out of college. And if for some reason Paul had failed to understand the first twenty times Barker gave one of his lectures, there was always the opportunity to fully understand during the next thousand which followed over the years. Paul knew he should have left the company years ago, but laziness on his part and family financial commitments kept him there. And now that his salary was at a comfortable level and he had accrued a lot of vacation time, he knew he would likely be with the company for the long haul. Unfortunately, so would Barker.

So, he found himself twenty years as a successful engineer with the company, yet he still had to endure the same tired old rhetoric repeated ad nauseam. Barker insisted on treating Paul as well as his coworkers like they were still inexperienced novices. Everyone hated the man, from the most senior engineers to the young workers right out of college.

Most of the time, Paul simply ignored Barker and pretended to agree with everything he said during these lectures. But there were other times, times when the pressure was on, times when he felt like he was juggling more balls than a two-bit hooker, times when Paul was sure he was on the verge of snapping. Those were the times when Paul did his best to avoid Barker at all costs. He didn't trust himself in such situations, and with good reason.

His mother had always taught him to be true to himself, know himself, and see himself for who he was. As a result, Paul knew who he was and his capabilities. On the surface, he was by all appearances a law-abiding citizen, never arrested, never having so much as a speeding ticket. He was a husband, a father, and attended church regularly. On that surface, others perceived him as the perfect citizen, a clean-cut type of neighbor anyone in suburbia would be happy to know.

But at those times when he was honest with himself, he knew there was someone else, another Paul, who resided just below that surface, behind the mask he wore to fool the world. This Paul was a much more sinister version of himself. Paul had managed to keep this other Paul at bay for all of his life, but lately, he felt it was getting harder to do.

He had thoughts, terrible thoughts of doing horrible things to people who annoyed him. He even had unbelievably bloody, violent dreams, dreams he never told anyone. These were dreams he could barely believe he was capable of having. What Paul found particularly disturbing was the extreme satisfaction he found he was getting from these dreams. Maybe it was an age thing, or perhaps the pressures of life and work were wearing him down. He wondered if one day he would no longer be able to fight this inner Paul. Like the times when he had to listen to Barker and his lectures.

"Let me out," a voice whispered from somewhere deep inside Paul's brain. Paul recognized that voice; it was his voice, yet at the same time, not his voice. It was the sound of the other Paul. It occasionally would whisper those three words in an attempt to coerce Paul to bring him forward, but Paul knew that was his signal to try to force the other Paul back, which he now did.

He had no idea what Barker wanted with him today, but he knew this was one of those days when he would be better off avoiding the man. Paul could sense that other Paul, scratching from somewhere deep down inside, trying to work his way to the surface, attempting to claw his way out. At times like this, the sensation almost became unbearable.

Yet Paul knew he could never let that other self surface, never. If he did, he was sure he would end up either in prison or dead. Once, many years ago, Paul had looked in the mirror and stared into the haunting eyes of his inner self. It was then he had comprehended the complete blackness of this other being. No, that Paul could never be allowed to walk the earth.

Paul walked into Barker's office and found the man seated at his compulsively organized desk, feigning being busy as usual squinting at his computer monitor while hunting and pecking away on his keyboard with two arthritic fingers. On the wall to his right hung the chrome-plated shovel with the message, Ground Breaking 1973, a souvenir of the office building's construction.

"Take a seat, Erickson, and close the door. I need to talk to you about something important."

Paul closed the door and sat down in one of Barker's two guest chairs. Barker said nothing but continued to bang away at his keyboard. This behavior was another thing about Barker that drove Paul crazy. If Paul was in the middle of a project that required concentration and Barker either approached his desk or summoned him by phone, Barker expected him to drop everything and come rushing in immediately to answer his master's call. However, once in the office, Paul had to sit patiently and wait. It was a passive-aggressive game Barker liked to play. He acted like the lord of the manor, who was too busy to find the time to share his wisdom with his lowly peasant.

"Let me out!" The other Paul hissed somewhat louder. It momentarily caught Paul off guard and startled him. Somehow, Paul managed to maintain his composure.

After what seemed like an eternity, Barker finally began his rant. After sitting through so many of these, Paul knew the routine by heart. Barker would ramble on, and Paul could only respond with the occasional head nod, approving look, or agreeable grunt. He was not permitted to speak or react in any other way. If Barker stopped somewhere in his endless monologue to take a breath and Paul tried to say something, he'd be chastised and accused of trying to "talk over" his boss, which was ridiculous since Barker talked over everyone. The truth was, Dick Barker never had an actual conversation with anyone in his entire miserable life. He never talked with people, he just talked at people, and they were required to listen. Any response or attempt to converse in kind would be seen as an attack since it interrupted the flow of Barker's valuable thought process.

"Let me out!" The voice insisted. Paul was beginning to feel sweat droplets forming on the back of his neck, not because of any fear of what Barker might say, but because he had never encountered such resistance from the Paul that lived within.

Barker said, "Erikson, you know I greatly appreciate your hard work and all you do for the company and me. You come in here and get right to work. You don't play on your computer or smartphone. You don't waste precious company time socializing or blabbing with coworkers. You rarely take your full hour for lunch, and most days, you're in here long before starting time. If we have an emergency, you're willing to make arrangements and stay late or come in on the weekends. And during the day, you put your nose to the grindstone. You get more work done than anyone in this company, including all the other engineers and managers. I see this, and I appreciate it."

Paul thought, "Here it comes, the 'but' part of the lecture. He's just got me all lubed up good so he can get ready and shove it in. It's that old-school manager trick; lead with something positive to relax the victim. Then when you have lulled him into a false sense of security, stick in the knife and twist it.

"Let me out!" The voice shouted. Paul shifted uncomfortably in his seat. He could feel the other Paul getting stronger, forcing his way forward, and didn't know what he would do about it.

Somewhere in the distance, he heard Barker still prattling on, "I also understand that you have family commitments and responsibilities outside of work, and as a result, you are up and out the door precisely at 4:00 whenever possible. But that's where we have a slight problem."

"Bingo!" Paul thought. "The 'but' has made its way into the monologue, and now it's time for the insertion. B.O.H.I.C.A—Bend Over Here It Comes Again."

"Let me out, Paul. I can stop this," other Paul insisted. Paul was dumbfounded. The inner Paul had never spoken so directly to him, let alone call him by name. Something was very wrong. He could feel his control of this inner self slipping away.

Barker said, "You know we have a brand-new top management team in here sent down from corporate. Our president, vice president, and general manager are all new. These three are watching everyone, just waiting for someone to run afoul of their commandments so they can shake things up. Remember Paul; perception is reality."

Paul felt his anger beginning to rise. And there it was, that ridiculous cliche again, perception is reality. What idiotic business magazine or management seminar did Barker steal that phrase from anyway? Seriously? This clown needed some new material. The other Paul was getting closer now. Paul was sure if he had a mirror, he would not see his own eyes reflected but those of the other. And the longer he sat and listened to this moron, the less he wanted to resist his inner self's insistence.

"You know I have your back Erickson, as well as that of your coworkers. I'll be having this same conversation with each of them regarding their shortcomings next. You're my senior guy. That why I'm speaking with you first."

"Lucky me, I get to hear it first," Paul thought. "I'm so blessed. What the hell does he mean by my shortcomings?" The other Paul was struggling to break free now. Paul could feel his awareness fading as the other made his way ever closer to the surface.

"Here's the thing, Erickson, there's a new sheriff in town, and he has two new deputies. They have to do something to show they are worth the exorbitant salaries the company pays them. They have to shake things up a bit, and they're watching all of us very closely. They've already told me they noticed you rushing out of here every day at 4:00 on the dot, and as a result, they assume you're a clock watcher who never gives the company more than required. Remember, perception is reality.

"I'm just watching out for you, Erickson. As a result, I'll expect you to stay fifteen minutes or so later every day so that their perception can change for the better. I'm not making a request either, Erickson; it's what I will require from now on. You'll have to figure out how to make this work with your personal life. Remember, perception is reality."

There was a momentary break in Barker's blabbing. It was that awkward place where Paul usually felt he was supposed to say something but knew if he did, Barker would jump on him for interrupting his runaway train of thought. But that was the old Paul Erickson, not the other Paul who had now made his way entirely to the surface.

"Is something wrong, Erickson?" Barker said with genuine concern, "You don't seem to be yourself."

In a disturbingly smooth, calm voice, Paul said, "I am myself; I'm finally my real self at last. I know how you and your kind perceive me, DICK, the same way you perceive everyone. People are nothing more than tools to be used to further your agendas."

"Wa . . . what?" Barker tried to ask. But before he could, Paul, the other Paul, took over.

"Shut up, Barker. You have nothing worthwhile to say. You never do, you never did, and you never will. All you ever do is open your bunghole of a mouth, flap your gums, and all that comes out is crap, the same crap day after day after day. You don't care about my coworkers or me. All you care about is saving your miserable job. Believe me, Barker, our jobs are a lot safer than yours. In your eyes, we may just be technical drones. However, if half the managers in this place disappeared tomorrow, no one would even notice. On the other hand, if my coworkers and I stayed home, this place would shut down. Think about it for a minute. We have to schedule our vacations so that no two of us are out at the same time. Otherwise, the world apparently would come to an end. So, the next time any higher up says anything about me leaving at 4:00, you tell him I said he could kiss my rosy, red ass."

"Erickson! I hope you realize I could have your job for this!" Barker screamed.

"No, you couldn't have my job because you can't do my job. You talk big and toss around buzz words pretending to know what you're talking about, but we all know better. None of you worthless management monkeys could ever even pretend to do my job. And you can't just place an ad in the newspaper and find someone else to do it either. Sure, I'm expendable; everyone is. But they'll miss me around here a lot more than you."

"Well, then I guess we'll see about that, won't we?" Barker said, "I've had it with your rudeness. You're fired, Erickson!"

"Well, that's the best news I've had all day, Dick. But unfortunately for you, I have other plans."

With that, Paul grabbed the celebratory shovel off the wall and rammed the pointed spade end in through his boss's mouth, pinning him against his chair, then twisting the shovel handle, he separated the top of his head from the bottom jaw. The severed portion of the head fell to the floor with a clunk. Paul Erickson rested the bloody shovel on his shoulders, then turned and walked out of Barker's office.

He strolled down the aisle between the half-walled partitions of his co-workers' cube farm while whistling a pleasant but unrecognizable tune. The other engineers had all heard the shouting coming from Barker's office and knew something terrible was happening in there. They were all popping up out of their cubicles like moles from holes, waiting and watching, assuming Barker had likely fired Paul. But they hadn't expected to see what they saw next. They all stared at Paul with his insanely happy face, whistling a happy tune while carrying a bloody shovel. A few of them looked back at Barker's office and saw the decapitated body slumped back in the chair.

As Paul left the office and pressed the elevator button to take him up to the executive level, one of the engineers said, "Oh my God, what should we do? Should we call 911?"

One of the senior engineers stepped forward. He had been as fed up with the corporate idiocy as Paul had been. He put his hand up in a stop gesture, smiled at the younger engineer, and said, "Let's give Paul a few minutes before we make that call. I suspect he has some more cleanup work to take care of upstairs first."

WELCOME HOME, CINDY

"When it's gone, you'll know what a gift love was.
You'll suffer like this. So go back and fight to keep it."
—Ian McEwan, *Enduring Love*

The whiskey shimmered in the light from the dwindling flame of the fireplace as he slowly moved the glass in small circles, allowing the amber liquid to flow over the ice cubes, which gently clinked against the side of the glass. As he sat in his recliner, Jonathan stared into the hypnotic fluid feeling as though there was another world, perhaps an entire universe waiting for him within the golden substance.

This love affair with alcohol had started as a nightly ritual several weeks after Cindy left, but it quickly increased to several times a day, and now drinking seemed to be something he did all the time. Jonathan suspected somewhere along the line he had become a full-fledged alcoholic, but he hadn't cared. Without Cindy, nothing had mattered. Perhaps now that he had gotten her back, he might be able to lay off the booze a bit, maybe not. He feared he might miss the way whiskey allowed him to relax, allowed his hyperactive brain to slow down. He supposed time would tell.

Thinking back, he had to admit to himself that leaving him wasn't entirely Cindy's fault. There were extenuating circumstances, which had led up to it. Perhaps he should even accept part of the blame himself. He recalled the intense argument they had while driving home from dinner the night she left him. She had accused him of criticizing several of her friends who joined them at the restaurant. She said he was "acting all high and mighty" and "always talking down to her friends" as if they weren't "worthy" of having a conversation with him.

He now realized Cindy probably did have a point. He did tend to belittle her choice of friends. But seriously, was it his fault he was born with a level of intelligence substantially higher than most people? Was it his fault that although they might be easy on the eyes, Cindy's girlfriends were, for the most part, boring airheads for whom any intellectual conversation was far beyond their scope of understanding? And was it his fault that he quickly became frustrated with attempting to tolerate those stupid bimbos. In Jonathan's ideal world, these women would be no more than child-bearing stock tied up in a barn, like cows awaiting fertilization.

Ok, so maybe from time to time, he was a bit overly infatuated with his ideas and, in turn, enjoyed hearing his voice expressing those ideas. But this was nothing new. Pontification was a way of life for Jonathan. He was the same way when he and Cindy first met. Back then, so many years earlier, she thought he was terrific. Cindy loved to hear his thoughts. She seemed to hang on every word he uttered. Somewhere along the line, something changed. He suspected she had been the one to change, as to the best of his observations, he hadn't.

Then he thought about one of Cindy's issues. It was a significant problem, which she hadn't ever taken the time to address. God knew he had pointed it out to her many times. She would never express her anger or frustration about something, which might be troubling her when it occurred. Instead, Cindy internalized everything. If something bothered her, she'd usually remain quiet about it and tuck it away somewhere deep inside. She would do this repeatedly until she had so much anger built up; she had no choice but to let it out.

Jonathan had experienced this with her many times. It was bizarre, and she could catch him entirely off guard if he failed to watch out for the signs. One day Cincy would seem fine. Then the next, she would scream at him for things he'd done, going back as far as a year earlier. She was like a volcano needing to let off steam from time to time.

Nonetheless, Jonathan accepted this about her. He had loved her as much as he supposed he was capable of loving anyone or anything. He sometimes suspected, especially towards the end, that he loved her more than she loved him. That was all right with him. He was smart enough to know how lucky he was to have someone as beautiful as Cindy was in his life. Hell, he was surprised any woman would want anything to do with a brainiac nerd like him, and Cindy had not only loved him and had married him.

As a result, whenever she had one of her moments and became angry or frustrated with him, he's simply let her vent. He learned early on in their relationship that trying to argue his point was a wasted effort, as it only served to make her angrier. He should have remembered that on the night she left him. It had been a mistake. Had he let her rant and get it off her chest, then things likely wouldn't have escalated the way they did, and she would never have left. But no, he had to argue back. He supposed all of that was irrelevant now that he had gotten her back.

He always knew he'd find a way to bring her back to him eventually. In the beginning, he struggled with how best to do it, and despite his intelligence, he never seemed to come up with the correct method. That was before he discovered the medicinal benefits of what he called his golden elixir of life, whiskey. Once he started imbibing, especially to excess, he could better focus his thought, and everything started to make more sense. Then one day, it all came to him like an epiphany. He knew what he had to do, and now that he had done it, his Cindy was back with him and would be forever.

Jonathan stood and walked across the room to the bed where his beloved Cindy waited for him. He didn't seem to notice the dirt and mud on his shoes and scattered all around the floor. None of that mattered to him anyway. All that mattered now was Cindy was back. As he shuffled closer to the bed, his foot kicked a tattered and yellowed old newspaper, which had been lying on the floor next to a discarded shovel. The paper flipped over, and the headline from over a year earlier jumped out from the front page. It read, "Woman Killed in Tragic Automobile Accident." But even had he seen the newspaper, Jonathan wouldn't have paid any attention to it.

Over the previous year, he had learned to put all of that behind him; how Cindy had gotten so angry with him that she had cursed at him and said she was going to divorce him. He had forgotten how she had slammed her fists into his face as they drove along that windy country road. And how he had lost control of the car and had gone off the roadway, crashing into a tree, killing Cindy instantly.

Yes, Cindy may have left him that night, and it may have caused him to go a bit crazy for a while, but he was fine now. With Cindy back home, things would be just like they were before.

"Welcome home, Cindy," Jonathan said as he crawled into bed and lay next to the cold, dead, decomposing corpse of his beloved wife.

WHITE ROOMS

"One creates from nothing . . . If you try to create from something,
you are just changing something. So, in order to create something,
you first have to be able to create nothing.

—WERNER ERHARD

He walked across the threshold, not surprised by what he found. After
all, he had walked into the same type of room dozens of times before.
So why would he be surprised?

The room was a perfect cube-shaped box, 12 feet long by 12 feet
wide by 12 feet high. There was an open doorway in the centers of
each of the four walls allowing access into four other identical rooms,
which led to four others, then more and then more: every one of them
the same.

The glass-smooth walls, ceiling, and floor of every room were completely white. The white was so brilliantly bright as to make it difficult
to see where the walls ended and the ceiling or floor began. The open
doorways were without moldings or any signs of boundary, and the
pure white room beyond the entrance, made them practically invisible
when viewed from straight on. There were no windows and no floor or
wall coverings of any sort.

How many of these empty white rooms had Jim experienced? How
long had he been walking from room to room? He didn't know. He did

understand a fact he had accepted about himself a long time ago was that he was dead. It was the only explanation, which made sense. He never was hungry or thirsty. He never needed to empty his bladder or bowels. He never slept, yet he was never tired. No living person of flesh and bone could make such a claim.

There were no mirrors in these rooms, so he couldn't see how he looked. However, Jim supposed he still looked as he had when he was alive. He could, however, look down and see his body. Jim wore a bright white linen shirt and pants but no shoes or socks. He could touch his arms and legs, and his hands didn't pass through him as he imagined they might if he was a spirit. However, Jim couldn't feel any sensation upon his attempted touch. Nor did he sense the smooth floor under his bare feet. He couldn't smell or taste anything either. It was all very surreal. He couldn't recall the circumstances, which might have caused his death, but he supposed that was a moot point anyway. Dead was dead.

What he didn't understand was what or where this place was. At first, he thought it might be Heaven, taking all of the bright white rooms into account. Yet why would Heaven be such a frustrating place where he walked from one vacant white room into another identical room? That seemed more like a type of Hell.

Perhaps that was the case. Maybe this was Jim's version of Hell. He had once heard that Hell was something unique to each individual. If so, then this particular version of Hell seemed fitting for one such as Jim. In life, he had been an artist, a musician, and a writer, gifted with a creative imagination. Yes, it seemed appropriate that his Hell would be one where he spent eternity alone, isolated and roaming from one desolate white cube of nothingness to another.

Then that sudden recollection, which for some unknown reason had eluded him since coming to this place, got him thinking. In life, he had always been a creative person. How could he have forgotten that? All of this time, Jim had been walking through so many empty rooms. He had trudged on like a zombie waiting for something to happen. But nothing ever happened. Then again, something never came from anything by itself. It took creativity to make that happen. In life, when Jim wrote a story or a song, he started with a blank page. When he drew or painted, he began with a blank sheet or canvas.

Then he wondered if he might still be able to use some of that creativity in this strange place. Perhaps it hadn't died with his body after all. Maybe it still resided in his soul but was only dormant, waiting for him to come back to awareness. The more he thought about it, the more it made sense. He realized it might be possible for him to think of each of these white walls as blank canvasses waiting for someone like him to breathe life into them.

He sat down on the floor in the middle of this latest room and stared at the wall directly across from him. He began to imagine a forest with trees of various shades of greens, browns, reds, and yellows. He thought of a stone path winding through the woods, starting where he sat and continuing to the open doorway. He imagined a variety of small woodland creatures inhabiting the forest.

Suddenly the walls began to change. All around the doorways, the walls displayed the most beautiful forest scene Jim had ever imagined. The trees weren't stationary. They swayed in a breeze, which even Jim could now feel. He realized this was the first he had felt moving air since coming to this place. Jim could even smell the fresh earthen scent of the woods. A shiny stone path of multiple colored round stones traveled from where he sat to the open doorway where it ended. Beyond the opening was another empty effervescent white room. He heard the twitter of birds and looked up into the trees to see them flying from one to the other. He saw a beautiful blue sky with puffy white clouds. He heard a chittering sound and saw squirrels and rabbits hopping along the ground and between the trees.

Jim reached down to place his hand upon the realistic-looking stone path, and to his surprise, he felt the shape and texture of the stones below. He picked up one of the stones from the ground. Jim turned the stone around in his hand, examining it closely. It appeared to be what he thought it should be. It was all so incredible. Somehow, all of his senses had returned to him.

He turned around and saw the entire room had become the forest of his imagination, and on each wall, the doorways led to additional white rooms. Jim stood and walked along the stone path to an entrance leading into one of the adjacent white rooms. As he passed into the room, he turned around to look at the room he had just left. To his surprise, he saw that the forest in the room itself was proliferating. It had tripled in size and was continuing to expand. The doorways began to disappear, becoming one with the forest.

Then the doorway he had just passed through vanished, replaced by a solid white wall. Looking around, he saw, only three more openings remained in the walls of this room. Once again, he sat on the floor in the middle of the room. This time he began imagining a sandy white beach along a beautiful blue ocean. He looked at the wall before him and saw large waves lapping along the shoreline. He could smell the fresh salty ocean air and heard seagulls soaring through the bright blue sky above him. He reached down and picked up a handful of sand mixed with various shell fragments and sea glass. It was amazing!

He realized he had been right from the beginning. This place must be Heaven. He had a limitless supply of rooms, which he could explore and use to create whatever he chose. It was an endless outlet for his creativity. Yes, indeed, this had to be Heaven.

Again, he stood up and walked through the doorway across the room in the center of the moving ocean waves. As before, as he stepped through the doorway, he turned to look back, and the ocean room was growing at a rapid rate. Once again, the door vanished, leaving him in a white room with three doorways. However, this time a man stood in the center of the room, dressed in a dark black suit with a black shirt and tie.

The man appeared older than Jim, with a head of long black hair combed backward hanging down to his shoulders, and he sported a pointed goatee. Jim realized this was the first person he had seen since coming to his place. There was an odd look in the man's eyes that Jim couldn't place.

"Who, who are you?" Jim asked.

"I am who I am, and you are who you are," the man replied cryptically.

"I mean, what's your name? And what is this place?" He tried again.

"Names are irrelevant. You are you, and I am I. And this place is what it is."

Jim was becoming frustrated with this line of non-productive conversation. "I guess what I want to know is . . . is this place Heaven, or is it Hell or perhaps somewhere else entirely?"

"What do you want this place to be?" The man inquired.

"I, I don't know exactly. I thought it might be a type of Hell for a long time because I was wandering from one room to another. Now I just learned I could change the rooms with my thoughts and make them into something else. I just made a forest and an oceanfront. So maybe it's Heaven after all. But how is it that I was able to do such a thing?"

The man looked at Jim quizzically and said, "Why, it's simple. You're a creator. As such, you've just created. That's what creators do, is it not?"

"But what exactly is it that I've created; a room, a stage setting, a diorama of sorts? What is it?"

"No, it's nothing as trivial as that. You've just created an entirely new world. You've created two worlds so far."

Jim was shocked. "What? That's impossible. I can't do such a thing."

"You may not have had that ability in life, but you do now. You've discovered your purpose in this place. You're now a creator of worlds. But I'm here to warn you of the dangers relating to your newfound abilities."

"Dangers?" Jim wondered.

"Yes, dangers. You have an extremely creative mind. If instead of creating beautiful worlds, let's say you chose to create a world of death and desolation, a world that was teeming with monsters or savage horrors beyond the comprehension of most men."

"I'm not sure what you mean."

The man held up his hand and said, "I understand. You see, what I mean is, with great creative abilities comes great responsibility. Your imagination in this place now has the potential of affecting the entire cosmos."

Jim said with frustration, "Seriously? Please, I'm just a simple artist. I don't deserve or want that sort of responsibility. I didn't ask for this."

"We seldom do. Yet here we are."

"So where exactly are we? Heaven or Hell?"

The man waited for a beat, then said, "That too will be entirely up to you. In life, we create our own Heavens or Hells. These occur based on the decisions we make and the roads we travel. In death, it's much the same."

"I don't understand," Jim said, confused.

"Earlier, you thought you were in Hell because of all the boring white rooms. Now you think you're in Heaven because you have billions of blank canvases upon which to create. You've made this place, what you've made it. If you do well, you will have created your version of heaven. But if you were to imagine something terrible such as a scene from Dante's Inferno, that would be an entirely different story."

Jim thought about that for a minute, and as he did, the walls began to smoke and turn red.

"Easy there," the man warned as the walls returned to their original white. "Remember what I said. You're responsible for what you create and, as such, will be held accountable. You have the potential of creating many different horrendous worlds, but this place wouldn't permit that. You see, there are natural checks and balances, and as a result, there are repercussions."

"Repercussions?"

"Yes, repercussions. Say you were to create a world that was detrimental to the benefit of the cosmos, it would be possible that the doors of that room would slam shut with you inside, and you would spend your eternity in the horrible world you've created; as punishment."

"Oh my God, that's horrible. And why did you have to mention Dante? How could you have put such thoughts in my head? How can

I possibly hope to stop or control the direction my imagination takes? It's like telling someone not to think of the color blue or the number three. The more you try not to think about something, the more you do."

"I'm afraid that's up to you, my friend. This world is your eternity. You're the creator now. You are the one responsible."

"Why, that's not fair. Who are you anyway? It's like you want me to fail."

The odd stranger just smiled a sly and devious grin. Jim suddenly realized this bizarre man was not what he seemed. He was more powerful in this place than Jim had understood, and he had set Jim up. First, the man had somehow allowed Jim to be bored and frustrated. Then he permitted him to recall his creative abilities and to form two new beautiful worlds. Then before Jim had a chance to build more, the deceiver had suggested Jim think of those same horrible things he was supposed to avoid.

A second later, the man disappeared, and Jim found himself alone once again in the white room. He was suddenly overwhelmed. He had no idea what he was going to do. He tried to think of smooth flowing streams and star-filled nights, birds, unicorns, and dancing elves.

But all he could imagine were fiery pits filled with damned souls tortured by scores of pitchfork-wielding demons. The walls around him began to redden and smoke as the stench of sulfur filled the room. Jim could hear the sounds of millions of lost souls screaming in agonizing torment. Jim cursed his imagination and wished his senses would once again go numb. He could feel the soles of his feet beginning to blister as unbearable heat and pain began to spread throughout his body. Try as he might, he couldn't reverse the transformation occurring to the room before him.

He thought to himself as the room began to expand and the doorways disappeared, "Looks like this place was Hell after all."

CHAINS OF LOVE

"These chains of love won't let me be."
—GERRY GOFFIN AND CAROL KING

How could he have done such a thing to her, and with a woman Maggie had considered to be her best friend no less? The entire matter sounded as cliché as the plot of some bad country-western song. She was beyond disgusted, beyond furious. Maggie always felt she and Roland would be together forever; that's how things were supposed to play out. But now, after what he and Angelina had done, never!

Maggie knew there was only one solution; only one way for her to get satisfaction; those two were going to have to die. She had already begun formulating a plan to get her revenge. It took her some time to prepare, but now everything was in place and ready to go. A small nook was in the stone-walled cellar of her old home, one she had realized was just big enough to hold two upright human bodies. At first, she knew what she wanted to do but had no idea how to make her plot a reality. So, Maggie did what she always did in such situations; she researched on the internet and, of course, found her answers.

At the local home center, Maggie purchased an electric hammer drill with a half-inch diameter masonry bit, several eyebolts, several small bags of quick-setting concrete mix, a trowel, and most importantly, six lengths of heavy-duty steel chain.

Drilling four deep holes high up on the stone wall was quite a chore for someone of Maggie's small stature. But to her relief, mixing a small amount of concrete and filling the holes before pushing in the steel eyebolts proved to be a lot less work. While the concrete was setting, Maggie decided that she'd return to the home center and purchase the bricks she would need. She didn't know if she had enough of them to do the job. However, when the back end of her compact hatch-back sank, Maggie figured that was all her small car could handle. Besides, she knew she could always go back for more if she needed them.

Once the concrete had dried and she had tightly secured the bolts, Maggie fed the chain through the rounded eye portion on the bolts. That was when she realized she would have to buy a few padlocks to hold the chains in place. Not a problem; it just meant another trip to the home center. She also had done a rough calculation of how many additional bricks she needed and decided to pick up the remainder of those as well.

When she returned home, she looked over her project to make sure everything was ready. Then she decided to put the rest of her plan into motion. She had to call Roland and pretended to take the high road regarding their separation and his affair with Angelina. She invited them both for dinner a few days later, under the guise of wanting to wish them both well in their new lives together. She planned to drug their drinks, rendering them unconscious. Then she hoped to drag their bodies down to the cellar. She wasn't sure she had the strength to do so, but if not, she'd pull them to the top of the stairway and let gravity do the rest. If they got hurt on the way down, so be it. Next, she was going to chain them together in the alcove, face to face if possible. Building a wall of bricks, she would seal the cheating couple inside. As far as she was concerned, they could remain chained together in there for eternity.

At first, she feared they might refuse her invitation, but to her pleasant surprise, the pair had accepted and had agreed to show up for drinks and dinner. However, during dinner, Maggie soon learned things hadn't turned out exactly how she had planned.

"You didn't think you could get away with whatever you have planned, did you?" Roland asked.

"Get away with what? I don't know what you're talking about," Maggie said with mock confusion. "Look, I invited you both to dinner to let you know there are no hard feelings and that I wish you well."

Angelina said, "I don't believe you, Maggie. We've both known you for a long time. Hell, I've known you since childhood, and this simply isn't your way. You're never happy unless you're getting even."

"Angie's right Maggie. Forgiveness isn't your way. Look, we both realize what we've done to you was probably the most despicable thing anyone could do, but we couldn't help it. Angie and I love each other; it's as simple as that."

Maggie struggled to maintain her artificially calm demeanor when, all the while, she wanted to grab a steak knife off the table and shove it to the handle deep through Roland's eyeball and into his deceitful brain. Hearing him referring to that bitch Angelina as "Angie" was enough to make her want to puke her guts out. Maybe after she had the couple chained up, she'd still shove that steak knife into Roland's brain. Then his precious Angie could slowly die of thirst and starvation dangling just inches from her lover's rotting corpse. Her lips would be practically pressing against the icy, stinking flesh of his face. It might take days for her to die. By then, the stench of decomposition would be overwhelming for her. Maggie decided she'd have to give that idea some serious consideration.

Maggie said insistently, "Look, both of you. I'm telling you I'm ok now. Yes, at first, I was hurt. And yes, I was originally furious. But now it's all over, and I've gotten past it. I don't have any intention of pretending that we can ever be friends again. That frankly is never going to happen. You both have done the unthinkable, but that doesn't mean I can't be the adult here and at least offer the olive branch of peace and be civilized about things. As far as I am concerned, after tonight we can all part company. I never want to see either of you again for the rest of my life. But for now, let's just eat, drink and forget everything else, at least for a little while longer."

Maggie noticed the couple exchanging glances which made her feel very uncomfortable. It was as if some unspoken thought had just passed between the two, something Maggie was did not understand.

"But what about what my cousin Dave said, Roland? Ask Maggie about that," Angelina said with blatant suspicion.

Once again, Maggie's temper started to rise to the surface, threatening to overtake her. Then once again, she managed to force the dragon of anger back into its cave. She'd have plenty of time and an infinite number of ways to show her fury when she had these two chained in her cellar.

She calmly said, "What about Dave, Angelina?" Although Maggie had referred to her friend as Angie thousands of times in the past, she no longer seemed to be able to do so, not after she heard Roland say that name. The sickeningly sweet tone of his voice when he said "Angie" was enough to cause diabetes.

Roland explained, "Dave works over at the home center, and although you never noticed him, he saw you come in several times the other day, and he saw what you bought."

"So what? I bought some supplies."

Angelina said, "Dave told us some of the stuff you bought looked a bit suspicious. He thought you might be up to no good or something."

"Seriously? Up to no good? An innocent woman buys some items for a home project, and suddenly she's public enemy number one?" Maggie asked, "Maybe I need make a call over to the manager of the home center and see that your nosey cousin Dave gets the reprimand he deserves."

Then with evident frustration in her voice, Maggie said, "Look, this whole dinner was a bad idea. I thought it might work out, but I should have known better. Do you know what I think? I think you two deserve each other. What say we just finish our drinks and call it a night?"

Roland agreed, and the three finished their drinks. No one spoke; they just sipped their glasses as their eyes traveled back and forth in furtive glances, as if in anticipation of something to come. Maggie found herself every bit as suspicious of the two as they were of her. She knew they certainly had a right to be wary even though she was confident they were unaware of the horrors she would rain down on them very soon.

"These drinks tasted a bit odd to me, Maggie," Roland said, glancing over at Angelina, "How about yours, Angie? Did yours taste a bit unusual?"

"Yeah. Yeah, it did, Rolli," she agreed. Both of the lovers were still wearing those strange, almost knowing expressions.

"Rolli?" Maggie thought, "She just called him Rolli? Good Lord! I honestly think I might puke after all." But instead of commenting, she assured them, "The drinks are fine. Mine taste just right."

"You know what I think, Rolli? I think this psycho bitch drugged our drinks," Angelina said with growing anger.

Roland looked sternly at Maggie and asked, "Maggie. That's not true, is it? You wouldn't try to drug our drinks, would you?"

Maggie waited a moment, then deciding the time was right, said, "Of course I did, you stupid, worthless toad. I drugged both of you. You'll both be out cold in a few seconds. But believe me, that's nothing compared to what I have in store for you both, very soon."

Angelina asked, "And what's that, Maggie? You mean your plan to chain us up in your cellar and then seal us in behind a brick wall to die?"

Maggie was stunned, "Wa . . . what? How do you? You can't possibly know?"

Roland said, "I told you, Maggie, Angie's cousin Dave works at the home center. He called and told us all about what you bought. We came over during your last trip to the store, and we checked out your little project in the cellar. I still have my house key, Maggie, or did you forget?"

"But, but, how . . ." Maggie was starting to feel strange as if the room was slowly spinning. Her eyelids were getting heavier, so heavy she couldn't hold them open.

///

When Maggie was finally able to open her eyes, she had trouble focusing. Her head hurt terribly, and she could hear an off-key female singing some song she recalled her mother singing when she was a little girl. Maggie wondered which band had recorded that song. She had no idea why she was hearing it now, although she did recognize Angelina's voice. Suddenly Maggie's eyes came into focus and saw a brick wall being slowly constructed just a few inches before her face. She tried to move her arms but found she was wearing the same chains she had planned for Roland and Angelina.

On the other side of the wall, she saw Roland busy adding brick after brick to the wall and placing generous slabs of cement between each one. Angelina was dancing around behind him with a half-empty bottle of vodka in her hand. She kept singing that same song over and over. Suddenly Maggie recognized the tune. Then, despite realizing the finality of her situation, Maggie couldn't help but appreciate the irony that "Chains of Love" would be the last song she ever heard.

INSANITY

"In individuals, insanity is rare; but in groups, parties,
nations and epochs, it is the rule."
—FRIEDRICH NIETZSCHE

"Insanity—a perfectly rational adjustment to an insane world."
—R. D. LAING

"Insanity is the final surrender."
—MARTA CAMINERO-SANTANGELO

"I guess if everybody went crazy together, nobody would notice."
—CORMAC MCCARTHY

/ 1 /

The previous months seemed endless with day-after-dreary-day dark
clouds, ceaseless rain, and damp chill air. It had been one of the
gloomiest springs and summers in recorded local history with hardly a
single full day of sunshine over the past six months. But now, finally,
the sun had managed to slice its way through the gloom. If even if only
for a brief time, it had succeeded in illuminating the city park over this
much-needed lunch hour with all its radiant glory.

Tad Dresden sat on the park bench, eyes closed with his face pointed directly upward into the brightness, absorbing every luminescent ray the sun could provide. He had chosen to sneak out a few minutes early and beat the crowd of what likely would be several hundred people once the clock struck noon. He had followed the weather forecast and knew this brief teaser of sunshine would be short-lived. The forecast said the rain would resume by 2 pm, with no end in sight. He might even extend his lunch hour a bit past one to enjoy the sun while it lasted. After all, his boss was on vacation in Florida and would have no idea if he did.

He couldn't blame his boss for skipping town for a while. Tad wondered how much more of this constant rain he could take as he had so many times during the past months. He and many of his coworkers had questioned at what point the never-ending gloom would drive them all crazy.

"You might not want to get too used to that sunshine, my friend. From what the weatherman says, it ain't gonna last much longer," an elderly-sounding voice said from nearby.

Not opening his eyes or changing his position, Tad replied, "That might be true, but I still plan on soaking up as much Vitamin D as possible, thank you very much."

"Nobody can blame you for that," the voice said with a chuckle, and Tad noticed the sound of the man's footfalls getting further away. He hoped he hadn't come across as rude or unfriendly. After all, the man had only been trying to strike up a conversation. But this was the first sunshine Tad had felt in weeks, and he couldn't seem to pull himself away from it.

A few minutes later, he heard the sound of shuffling along the concrete path approaching him. At first, he thought it might be the previous stranger returning, perhaps to make another attempt at conversation. Tad hoped not, as all he wanted was to soak in more of this incredible sunshine. Then he thought, hadn't that stranger's footsteps sounded normal, like regular footfall? These didn't sound like normal footsteps at all, but we're more like an erratic dragging along the walkway. He suddenly realized just how vulnerable he was sitting there;

face pointed skyward with his eyes closed. Any mugger could walk up to him with a club, bash his skull to a pulp before he even had time to react. Even in this active part in a relatively safe part of town, there were no guarantees.

Tad heard a strange monotone voice coming from directly in front of him murmuring in some unknown language he couldn't begin to identify, "Mula roo. Wallama tang. Foona taloon."

He cautiously opened his eyes to see a strange man standing in front of him, not more than three feet away. He appeared to be in his mid-thirties with a receding black hairline already showing signs of gray. He wore dark brown dress pants, matching socks and shoes, a white shirt with a tan tie. At first glance, the man would have looked like any one of a dozen office workers out for a lunchtime stroll. That was except for the crimson stain on the front of his shirt and tie. Not to mention the bloody box cutter he held tightly in his right hand.

"Fargar muffta varnoff palantarf," the man jabbered incoherently. That was when Tad noticed the man's eyes for the first time. Somehow those eyes had simultaneously managed to alternate between dead and void of all emotion to the wild eyes of a vicious, crazed animal.

"Look, buddy," Tad said with a quivering voice, "I . . . I don't want any trouble." Tad wasn't a big man, only about 5-6 and 135 pounds soaking wet. He knew nothing about self-defense and had never been in a single fight in his entire life, but he sensed the threat level was about to go nuclear. Tad slowly brought his cellphone around, prepared to call 911 if the need arose. He thought a whole lot of good that would do him if this weirdo decided to go ballistic. If the wacko was so inclined, he could slice Tad to ribbons long before any cops arrived.

To Tad's surprise, the man didn't attack, however, nor did he respond in any way to the attempts Tad made to calm him. It was like he hadn't heard a single word Tad had spoken. He just stood staring wide-eyed as a broad Jack-O-Lantern grin began to spread across his face. Tad ventured a glance down at his smartphone and pressed the telephone icon.

Then to Tad's horror, the man lifted the blood-splattered box cutter and placed the tip of its razor edge against his forehead at the place

where flesh met his thinning hairline. Tad grimaced in stunned disbelief as the man sunk the blade a quarter of an inch into his forehead,
not so much as flinching from what had to be an incredible level of
pain. Tad felt the phone fall from his grip and clatter to the park bench,
but he was too shocked by what he saw to retrieve it.

Slowly the man dug the blade across his forehead, then down the
left side of his face as blood streamed over his now bulging eyes. Still,
the man smiled that ridiculous Cheshire Cat grin, blood tricking into
his lips. Somewhere in the back of Tad's mind, a voice was screaming
at him to find his phone, call 911 and get away from the maniac as
quickly as possible. Yet he sat staring, transfixed.

The man's lips were in constant silent motion. Tad was sure the
stranger must still be murmuring those bizarre, unintelligible words.
When the blade had cut its way to just below the man's chin, he
repeated the process on the right side of his face, completing the maca-
bre bloody circle.

The stranger released the box cutter allowing it to clatter to the
pavement. He began gradually increasing the volume of his voice as he
lifted both of his hands toward his forehead. Tad's stomach churned
with disgust as the man dug his fingernails deep into the groove he had
sliced into his forehead.

"Mongoda denolla avatar yulunda!" The man screamed as he
began peeling down the flesh from his face, pulling it off in one piece
like some hideous latex mask. Tad heard ripping sounds as flesh separated from musculature. As he looked on in disbelief, he saw the man's
crimson under-face revealed. The stranger tossed the skin mask aside,
shouting, "Dura haarmazolla! Dura haarmazolla!"

Before Tad could react, if he was still even capable of responding,
the now faceless madman turned and ran screaming across the nearby
grassy park for a few dozen yards before collapsing to the ground, lying
face down. His body twitched and convulsed for a few moments, then
became motionless. Tad had never seen a man die before and most
certainly not in such a revolting self-inflicted manner. He sat staring in
awe at the unmoving mass of tattered humanity lying on the ground
before him.

A series of tremors began somewhere deep inside Tad's stomach and quickly spread throughout his body in ever-increasing intensity, like ripples of water radiating from the epicenter of a rock dropped in a pond. He heard someone screaming a series of unintelligible gibberish words, and as he felt a slow stream of drool trickling down his chin, he realized the voice he heard was his own.

/ 2 /

About thirty feet across the park, an attractive, professionally dressed woman named Emma Larson stopped in her tracks, staring in confusion at the man on the park bench. At first glance, he appeared to be a typical office worker dressed in the shirtsleeves and tie uniform she had seen thousands of times. But there was nothing ordinary about the way he was acting. The man, mumbling to himself, quaked from head to toe as if in convulsion. Emma had encountered more than her share of crazy homeless street people in her life, but this character didn't seem to fit that profile.

She saw him staring off to the left, and following his gaze, she saw another man lying in a heap on the nearby grass. That man was motionless, and at first, he appeared to have a red cloth draped over his face. Then Emma saw the crimson stains on his shirt and realized the man was dead. What she thought to be a red cloth was no cloth at all but the man's face. And what had happened to him? He looked as though someone had beaten him to a pulp. Perhaps it had been that shivering man sitting on the park bench. Maybe he had hit the other man or shot him in the face. Could that be? Emma quickly took cover behind a large oak tree and fished her cellphone from her purse with trembling fingers.

Emma quickly keyed 911, desperate to hear the operator's voice. She peeked around the tree, venturing a look back at the man on the park bench. To her shock, he was now staring back at her. He raised his right arm, pointed directly at Emma, and shouted, "Garnog mon dragoob balute!"

She remembered her phone. Why hadn't the 911 operator responded? She looked down and saw she had forgotten to press the call icon. She pushed it quickly as she looked back at the man on the bench again. He now was standing, and upon seeing her, he began running toward her rapidly driven by nothing short of madness. Emma had never seen another human running so fast and knew she could never outrun him. But she quickly learned he had no intention of chasing her; it was the tree she hid behind which caught his interest.

"Aronda mogolup grontach," the man screamed at the top of his lungs as he slammed himself face-first into the trunk of the tree. The man backed away and repeated the process, each time ramming his face harder and harder until it looked like a sagging pile of raw hamburger meat. After a few final attempts, the man slid down the tree, lying unconscious or dead at its base.

Emma dropped her phone to the grass and cautiously walked around to the front of the tree. A ruby red accumulation of blood, hair, and bits of flesh coated its bark. Looking down at the man, she saw his skull had cracked open and gray matter slowly dribbled out onto the grass.

In the distance, she heard a faint voice saying, "911 operator. What is the nature of your emergency?"

Emma didn't respond. She didn't hear. She couldn't hear. She was too overwhelmed by the sounds coming from her mouth. They were words she had never heard before, if they were words at all. At first, they seemed like nonsensical gibberish until they weren't.

/ 3 /

"What the hell is going on over there?" Sam Hartley said to his friend Kevin.

Kevin, who was a far cry from observant, asked, "Over where?"

"Over there by that park bench," Sam said with annoyance. "Something weird is going on. I think we should go check it out."

"What are you talking about, Sam? There's nothing weird going on. It looks to me like some woman is sitting on the ground by a tree. What's the big deal?" Then Kevin's voice took on a sinister tone. "Oooh, look out, everybody. Some scary secretary is out sitting under a tree enjoying the first sunshine we've had in months. What sort of unspeakable horror is she busy conjuring? Maybe she'll terrorize the world by eating a peanut butter and jelly sandwich. Oh, the horror! Oh, the humanity!"

"Ok, I get it, Kevin. Your sarcastic wit has not fallen on deaf ears. But tell me what that is next to her. It looks like a man lying on his back; maybe he's dead."

"Oh yeah, I'm sure. Every person lying in the grass enjoying the sunshine is dead. Sam, you better do something about that wild imagination of yours."

"Fine, Kevin, fine. I know I have an active imagination—big freaking deal. You can say whatever you want, but I'm telling you, something weird is going on over there. I'm going over to see what's what."

"Knock yourself out, Sammy boy. I'll be sitting here on my bench, soaking in rays and relaxing. After you've discovered that all of this was in your head, come back, and we'll enjoy the rest of our lunch hour."

Sam walked across the park toward the woman under the tree. As he got closer, he heard what sounded like the distant, tinny voice of someone speaking over a phone. It was coming from the grass, not far from the woman. Then he heard the woman herself, almost chanting in some strange dialect he has never heard before.

She slowly rocked back and forth, mumbling in her bizarre language, "Quavilla esto monalinko dazaflog."

As he reached the woman, Sam noticed the other body lying in the grass. It appeared to be that of a man, but Sam couldn't be sure, as the thing's face was unrecognizable. Even its head was cracked open, and its brains pooled in the grass. Sam could hear the buzzing of hundreds of blowflies, making him wonder what sort of communication allowed them to find death so quickly.

In the distance, he saw yet another body, this one was as faceless as the last, but it appeared less damaged than the other. Sam didn't know why, but for some reason, he thought of facial surgery. Then he noticed the buildings across from the park disgorging what looked like hundreds of workers who had chosen not to skip out a bit early as he and Kevin had. They were about to get the shock of their lives.

What in the hell was going on? What had happened to these people, and why was this woman sitting alone, mumbling? That was when he noticed the two blackbirds bouncing through the grass toward the woman.

One of the birds pecked at something lying in the woman's open palm. Sam's stomach clenched with disgust as he saw the bird hop away with a human eyeball dangling from the muscles and filaments it held tightly in its beak. The orb swung back and forth like a pendulum, dripping tiny droplets of blood in its wake. Sam released an audible gasp, and the woman turned to face him.

She shouted her gibberish now, "Mololla dero Banga harawan!"

That was when Sam saw the hollow black and crimson orifices that had once held the woman's eyes. Deep furrows dug into her cheeks ran down from the empty sockets acting like tributaries for the blood streaming down her ruined face. The woman's non-seeing face turned toward the sound of Sam's presence, and as she broke into a large, happy grin, her hands reached up, fingers sliding inside her mouth, each hand grabbing tightly onto the bottom jaw. With the sound of breaking bones serving as the soundtrack for this heinous ballet of the bizarre, Sam watched in paralytic horror as the woman began twisting and tearing at her lower jaw. At first, she broke it free of its physical moorings, then eventually pulling it entirely away from her face itself in a flurry of torn flesh, broken bones, and a shower of blood.

She fell sideways, collapsing to the ground in a heap as Sam reached her. But there would be no assistance he could render. She convulsed for a few seconds then all movement ceased.

Sam began to cry, something he hadn't done since he was a kid. He whispered a prayer, which was something else he hadn't done in longer than he could recall. But partway into his plea, his words became a garbled mess of incomprehensible babbling.

/ 4 /

As Kevin sat meditating, he heard a growing series of noises coming from the park's far end. He couldn't make out what anyone was saying, but he knew that something terrible was happening by the tone of the voices. Concerned about what sort of trouble his friend Sam might have gotten himself into, Kevin looked out in the distance and was staggered by what he saw. There were dozens, no hundreds of people in the park, all screaming, waving their arms, and attacking each other. People were punching, kicking, and gouging each other in some of the most violent acts Kevin had ever imagined. Many of the people appeared to be inflicting pain upon themselves as well. He saw people tearing the flesh from their faces. He saw others ripping arms out of people's sockets then using them as clubs to beat more people.

It was complete insanity. It was the sort of thing Sam might imagine but not Kevin. Not only did his thought never travel to such places, but he was having great trouble wrapping his head around the reality he was now seeing. Sam was out there amid that horror, and Kevin had no way of finding him. What in the hell could have caused so many people to lose their minds and begin slaughtering each other, not to mention maiming themselves?

As he turned to run, Kevin said to himself, "Ok. I may not be smart enough to know what's going on over there, but I do know if I want to stay alive, I have to get out of here and pronto. Maybe if I can get far enough away, I can call . . . I can call . . . I . . . ironda maradunga banadogo. . . ."

DEAD PUMPKINS

In the minimal illumination from a streetlight, two boys stood staring at what was on the house's front porch. Things were not as they should have been.

"What the heck's that supposed to be?" Eric asked Charlie, whose mouth was agape at the rotting mess before him.

"Don't know what it is, but I know what it was the last time I saw it."

"You told me this house had the biggest coolest pumpkin in the whole town. Does this look like the biggest or coolest pumpkin to you? It looks like a pile of crap to me."

"I'm telling you, Eric, when I first saw this thing, it was huge and bright orange, carved real cool with a candle inside. It was awesome, I'm telling you."

"Yeah? Well, it don't look so awesome now. It looks like a pile of rotted pumpkin poop now, Charlie."

The two boys were on their annual Halloween quest to steal pumpkins from neighbors and smash them into pieces. This event was what they called was their "Dead Pumpkins" ritual. They were hoping to break last year's record of twenty. They were within one pumpkin of shattering that record.

This pumpkin was not only supposed to be record-breaking but the crowning achievement of their Dead Pumpkin adventures. It would put the boys far ahead of those geeks, Sam Williams and Billy Martin, who were determined to kill more pumpkins than Eric and Charlie this year. This pumpkin was supposed to be the one to beat them all. At least that's what Eric thought, based on what Charlie had said. Now he was wondering if they could even count this as an official pumpkin.

Eric stared in disgust at the shriveled, withered, and moldering mess sagging on the porch, barely able to stay upright on the makeshift stand. The majority of its orange color was gone, replaced by patches of black on its base and brown, yellow, white, and green rot. The once carefully carved face of the pumpkin now sunk inward; its open mouth looked like an old toothless crone.

"I wonder what the heck happened to this thing? I'm telling you, Eric, only yesterday this was the coolest pumpkin I even saw."

Eric stared at the mess for a few minutes, then sighed with frustration. "Well, it looks like we have to find another pumpkin to be our record-breaker. I don't know. This one's just a big glob of pumpkin snot."

"Can't we still count this one if we take it and smash it?" Charlie wondered. "I mean, think about it. After it's smashed on the ground, who'll ever know what it looked like?"

"We'll know. Besides, look at that thing. Who'd want to pick it up? Our hands would sink right into that mess," Eric wore a look of disgust.

Charlie suddenly had an idea. "I've got gloves. I could wear them to pick the thing up."

"If you want to try, you can, but those gloves won't be worth squat by the time you're finished."

"Don't worry. My mom can put them in the wash, and they'll be as good as new."

"Your mom just might beat your sorry butt if you bring gloves home covered in pumpkin puke."

"Don't sweat it, Eric. I got this."

Charlie put the gloves on, then slowly and carefully. He reached out to the rotting mound and put one hand on each side. He feared the thing would collapse in on itself, so gingerly began to lift the pumpkin, feeling as if he was Indiana Jones raising a golden idol from its resting place in some ancient cavern.

When the decaying pumpkin was level with his face, it began to pulsate slightly. Charlie thought it might be more rotten than he'd anticipated. It could turn into a messy lump in his hands, ruining his gloves forever. If that happened, Eric was right; his mother would kill him for sure. Then he realized his hands weren't sinking into the pumpkin; it was changing.

He stood speechless in shocked terror, the blackened pumpkin molding itself into another shape; a hideous grinning skull. Charlie was paralyzed with fear as two giant bulging eyeballs appeared in the hollowed-out sockets. They were looking directly at him with evident hunger.

Eric watched the impossible events unfolding before his eyes. His best friend stood helplessly staring at the grinning rotten specter he held in trembling hands. Eric reached out to grab Charlie, hoping to get him to drop things, but as soon as Eric touched his friend's shoulder, he too became as petrified as a statue. He didn't know what would happen to them next, but he knew he was helpless to do anything to stop it.

The skull/pumpkin opened its mouth to an impossible size. A vile stench came out from somewhere inside the horrid thing. Then the two terrified boys were drawn toward the gaping maw. Moments later, the boys disappeared inside the Hell-born demon's mouth, among the screams of terror and crunching bones.

The skull began to morph back into a pumpkin shape. It was no longer a rotting mess of decaying remnants. It had returned to its original, beautiful large, bright orange countenance.

"There it is," Billy Martin shouted.

Sam Williams agreed, "Yeah. It's amazing. I'm so glad you spotted it. We'll destroy Eric and Charlie's record this year for sure."

"I wonder why those two idiots didn't make it here ahead of us," Billy said.

"Who cares? We're about to become the dead pumpkin champs of the whole town. Let's grab that thing, Billy."

HE KNOWS WHEN YOU'RE AWAKE

Patience wasn't among those virtues young Timmy France could claim as his own. At eleven years old, Timmy seemed to have even less patience than he had back when he was much younger. This lack of patience was especially true when it came to birthdays or, more importantly, Christmas.

Although he no longer believed in Santa Claus, his elves, or his flying reindeer, Timmy kept this secret from his parents. He felt telling them might somehow ruin Christmas for them. It seemed important to them that he still believed, so he played along.

Timmy looked forward to Christmas every year, especially getting presents. He loved guessing about what his parents had brought him, but he hated the waiting. As soon as the gifts appeared under the tree on Christmas Eve, Timmy was ready to tear them open. However, his parents would never allow such a thing. They had a strict set of rules regarding the holiday. One of those rules was he had to wait until Christmas morning to open his presents.

He sometimes wondered if the reason his parents, especially his father, wanted him to believe in Santa was that it gave them one more way to make sure he did whatever they wanted. His dad would often use all the standard Christmas threats against him, such as "Bad boys get coal in their stockings," or "He sees you when you're sleeping, he knows when you're awake." As if this wasn't bad enough, his father felt the need to take these threats to a much higher and, unfortunately, much more disturbing level for some unknown reason. Timmy had no idea why his father insisted on doing this.

He recalled the first time his father had told him one of his strange tales. He had been a boy of four or five, and it still bothered him to think about it.

"You know, Timmy," His father had said, "Most people only know about the good side of Santa Claus and his elves. You know how he brings toys and candy to good boys and girls."

"Yeah, I know, Daddy."

"But nobody ever talks about what happens to the bad kids, do they?" Timmy had said nothing.

Then his father asked, "Do you know what happens to bad boys and girls at Christmas time, Timmy?"

Timmy hesitated for a moment, then reluctantly said, "You told me Santa brings the bad kids coal."

"Oh no, no, Timmy. It's much, much worse than that. You see, Santa is magical. Do you know what that means?"

"Yes, Daddy, I know what magic is."

"Well, it means Santa can change into whatever sort of creature he wants to if he needs to punish a bad little boy."

"I, I don't understand, Daddy. What do you mean?" Timmy said uncertainly.

"Well, let's say some little boy breaks one of the Christmas rules like maybe the little boy doesn't go to sleep early on Christmas Eve. You know that's one of our rules, right Timmy?"

"Yes, Daddy."

"Well, if Santa finds out, he might turn himself into an ugly old monster then come into the boy's house and smash all of his presents."

"That would be mean!" Timmy argued.

"Yes, it most certainly would be. Or maybe if the little boy was really naughty, Santa might turn his elves into trolls. You know what trolls are, don't you, Timmy."

"Yes, Daddy. They're horrible monsters."

"They sure are. And these trolls would capture the boy and carry him away to eat for dinner."

Timmy's mother had shouted at her husband, "Bob, stop that now! You'll terrify the boy!"

"Better that he be scared, Margaret, then end up in the cookpot of some horrible troll."

Timmy had been horrified by his father's story. Timmy conjured up an image of jolly old St. Nick transforming into some kind of monstrous horned demon and his elves becoming hideous trolls, with his overactive imagination,

"So, Timmy. You have to make sure you never break any of our Christmas rules. I would hate to think what Santa would do to you if you did. To make matters worse, he might take it out on your mother and me for not teaching you the rules of Christmas. You wouldn't want that would you?"

These fear tactics had worked for several years, and Timmy always made a point of doing exactly as his parents told him. That was until Timmy stopped believing. Once that happened, he no longer feared demonic Santa or fanged elves. If there was no Santa, there was no threat. However, he never let his parents know that he was aware the tales were nothing more than a bunch of nonsense.

Now that he was eleven, Timmy decided things should be different. This year he had formulated a plan. Timmy decided to pretend to be terrified while his dad spewed his annual stories about demonic Santa and his cannibalistic elves. Then he'd wait until his folks were asleep, and he'd slip downstairs to check out his presents. He figured he'd start with his stocking since returning it to its original state would be easiest. Most of the time, his mom just crammed stuff into the Christmas stockings with no rhyme or reason.

The wrapped gifts would be a bit trickier. Timmy would try first to look through the paper using his flashlight to see what waited beneath. He knew some of the presents might involve his opening one end to see what was inside. If necessary, Timmy could use some transparent tape to refasten the paper. His folks would never be the wiser.

On Christmas Eve, Timmy lay awake in his bed, fine-tuning his plan. He waited for a full hour after his parents went to bed before getting ready to go downstairs. As Timmy sat on the edge of his bed with his feet resting in the warm carpet, he heard a strange noise coming from his parent's bedroom. He didn't recognize the sound, but it was so unusual that it caused an icy chill to skitter down the middle of his back momentarily.

At first, he had thought he heard a growling noise, then a thumping sound followed by a gasp. He sat silently for several minutes, listening for the noise again, but it never came. Thinking he must have imagined it or else it was just his father tossing in his sleep, Timmy slowly opened his door and crept past his parents' bedroom.

Usually, by this time of night, he could hear his father's snoring; the man had a snore that could rattle the floorboards, but tonight he was sleeping soundlessly. His mother always slept without making a sound, and tonight was no exception. Cautiously, Timmy walked down the stairs, careful to keep to the outside edges of the stair treads. He had learned this trick from a detective move he had watched several weeks earlier. It was supposed to keep the steps from squeaking. He reached into his pajama pants pocket, took out his small Maglite, and shone it on the area in the living room where he knew the Christmas tree stood.

On the floor, at the base of the ornately decorated tree, Timmy saw a Christmas stocking with his name embossed in raised glitter lettering. His mother had made it for him years earlier. The bottom part of the Y at the end of his name had worn off over the years. Regardless, he had always thought it was the most beautiful stocking he had ever seen. He recalled how she had told him Santa and his elves had made it especially for him. Seeing his stocking always made him feel special. He looked around to make sure neither of his parents had awoken or had heard his creeping. He was still alone. He slowly approached his stocking, and after another glance around the room, he bent down for a closer look.

Timmy lifted the stocking and reached deep down inside, having not noticed how the bottom was darker in appearance than the rest. He was far too eager with anticipation of what he might find. When his hand reached the bottom, he suddenly got an uneasy feeling in the pit of his stomach as his fingers touched something warm, sticky, and wet.

At first, Timmy thought perhaps His mom had put a chocolate bar in his stocking, and it must have melted. He once had a chocolate bar melt in one of his pants pockets, and it felt a lot like this. Yet this still felt different, warm, unlike anything Timmy had ever experienced before in his young life. He could feel something round and soft among the sticky wetness.

Timmy withdrew his hand and could see that his fingertips glistened with a sticky red substance with a strange coppery smell. He opened his hand, expecting to find a marshmallow based on its texture. Instead, what he saw, caused a scream of unbridled terror to catch in his throat as his stomach flipped in revulsion. Sitting in the palm of his hand floating in crimson gore was a single human eyeball.

He jumped up reflexively, shaking his hand to rid himself of the horror, wiping it on his pajama top. He began to tremble from head to toe. He tried to scream but was unable to do so. Involuntary tears were streaming down his face. His lips moved to form a cry for his mother, but no sound came.

Reacting without thinking, Timmy turned and ran up the stairs taking several of them at one time. When he burst into his parents' room, he stopped abruptly staring at the bed illuminated by the moonlight coming through the open window, revealing a horror beyond anything his young mind could have ever imagined. It was worse than his most graphic video game, worse than any horror movie he had ever seen.

His parents' bodies sprawled across their bed with the covers turned down. Their tattered and bloodied corpses were too intensely visible against the white bed sheet now splattered crimson. Likewise, blood had soaked their pajamas. His father's body was in a slightly sitting up position; his throat slit from ear to ear, looking like some hideous, toothless grin. It was also evident by the gaping black hole in his skull that one of his eyes was missing. Timmy knew where that eyeball was now.

"He knows when you're awake." A deep, gruff, guttural voice hissed from a darkened corner of the bedroom. "Oh, Timmy, Timmy. You didn't listen to your father, did you, Timmy? Instead, you insisted on breaking the rules. That makes you a naughty boy, Timmy. Bad boys must pay for breaking the rules."

Timmy stared into the darkened space as a creature slowly made its way into the moonlight. The thing was about four feet tall with long ape-like arms that hung down to the floor where Timmy saw two large hands with sharp claws. It wore a tattered green suit, ripped because it could no longer fit the muscular body of the elf, which had transformed into the beast before him. The thing's bulging hair-covered muscles glistened with sweat, and Timmy could smell a horrible stench coming from the monster.

"Santa is very upset with you, Timmy France, for breaking the rules. Your parents should have warned you, and you should have listened. He sent us to make things right. I'm sure when Santa sees the wonderful Christmas dinner we'll be bringing with us, he'll feel a lot better about things. You'll be our gift to him, Timmy. And after all, isn't giving what Christmas is all about?"

THE BEWILDERMENT OF HARRY EASTON

"Forty is the old age of youth; fifty the youth of old age."
—VICTOR HUGO

"Those who love deeply never grow old; they may die of old age,
but they die young."
—DOROTHY CANFIELD FISHER

The recliner-rocker moved rhythmically forward then backward, forward then backward; its slow relaxing motion controlled by Harry's right foot as always. His left foot was crossed over his right knee, forming a makeshift desk which he used week after week as he had done for the previous three decades. The television played a repeat episode of CBS Sunday morning, the volume adjusted loud enough for Harry to hear without affecting his concentration. The show was something about the increase in cases of elder abuse in nursing homes.

Since it was Sunday morning, it meant this was the day Harry sat down to pay his bills. Some people might suggest that it might be easier to perform this particular task at an actual desk. Or perhaps at a worktable away from distractions and interference, but not Harry. This method was when, where, and how he liked to do his bill paying. And it was the way he had done things since his twenty-second birthday. God, it was hard to believe he was fifty-three already.

Harry never paid his bills early; he always paid them right on time or as close to on time as was possible. He also paid them by check and through the good old US postal service. His son, Brad, tried to get him to set up automatic bill paying, but Harry would have none of that.

"I've always paid my bills this way, and I'm not about to change now," he would say.

Harry found this slow, manual bill-paying method relaxing, especially since he got to watch TV while doing so. As he sat, he felt a slight rumble in his stomach. Harry knew his wife, Eva, was upstairs getting a shower, so if he chose to let one rip, no one but the dog would be any the wiser. Harry was sure the dog wouldn't rat him out. He leaned to the right a bit to perform his tried and true one cheek sneak, and the air cracked with the sound of his eruption.

///

"Did you hear that?" The middle-aged nurse, Wanda, said to her nurse's aide, Maria. "Sounds to me like old Mr. Easton might have just left you another present."

"He better not have," the young aide replied, "He crapped himself like three times yesterday, and I had to clean him up. One time it leaked out, and I had to get two orderlies in here to lift his sorry butt up and out of bed while I changed the sheets. I wish they could shove a plug up his bunghole until the crap came out his ears."

The older nurse chuckled, "Wouldn't matter 'cause you'd still have to clean it up, even if it did pour out of his ears."

The aide turned a bit too quickly and bumped a utility cart, sending a metal bedpan crashing to the floor. The noise startled their sleeping patient.

"Eva? Eva? Are you alright?" Harry Easton called.

Maria said with frustration, "And there he goes again calling for his dead wife; like she gonna come waltzing in here after being worm food for the past . . . how many years is it?"

"She passed more than ten years ago," Wanda replied quietly, trying to calm her aide, "When she was seventy-three." Wanda knew Maria was quick-tempered, and she suspected the aid might be less than gentile with her patients when she became angry. The last thing their rest home needed was an investigation into elder abuse.

"Yeah, that's right. Ten years. And this old fossil still thinks she is alive and kickin'. How old is this character anyway, like eighty-something?"

"He's eighty-three. Now, Maria, I'd suggest you take a deep breath, relax and get hold of your temper. Ok? Then you can get Carlos and Raymond to come in here and give you a hand with Mr. Easton. Do you understand what I'm trying to say to you?"

"Um . . . yeah. Sorry, Wanda. I just got a bit carried away. I'll be fine now."

///

Harry swore he heard something fall upstairs. It had a metallic sound. He wasn't concerned about the noise since the master bathroom was right above him. It was likely that Eva had accidentally knocked a cup off the bathroom vanity. If Eva had fallen, the noise would have been much louder, especially since both of them could stand to lose twenty pounds or so. Besides, Eva always stomped on the floor, signaling with their code if she needed him.

He waited for a second for the stomp, but it didn't come. It could mean nothing, and all was well, which it probably was. But what if Eva had fallen and couldn't call to him or stomp on the floor. It wasn't like an old and feeble lady; she was a strong, capable woman, but still, Harry decided to call up to her.

"Eva? Eva? Are you alright?" He called but got no reply.

Although he was sure he was letting his imagination get the best of him, Harry decided he should probably take a walk upstairs and make sure she was ok. As he started to get up from his recliner, he began to feel strange, as if he was floating on air or lifted upward.

///

"Careful Ray," Carlos said, "I don't want to get that crap all over me like last time." The two orderlies were lifting Harry out of his bed to carry him to a waiting chair, the one covered with protective plastic.

Ray chuckled, "Yeah, that was pretty funny. I wouldn't mind seeing that again."

"I'll just bet you'd love that."

Harry was shocked to find himself suddenly being lifted by two large strangers. What the hell was going on? Where was his recliner? Where was his house? He looked down and noticed two hands resting on his lap. They were thin and frail in appearance, with almost translucent skin covered with liver spots. Whose hands were they? They weren't his, were they? He smelled something foul and was horrified to realize the stench was coming from him.

"Where's Eva? Who are you, people?" Harry cried in a weak, raspy voice, now thoroughly confused. He tried to fight against the two men holding him but found he didn't have the strength. He realized those pitifully elderly hands he had seen were his. But how could that be? He was just fifty-three years old a few seconds ago. How could he have aged thirty years in a few seconds?

"Easy old-timer," Raymond whispered into his ear. "You'd better take it easy and not get any of that stinkin' crap on me or believe you me; I'll make you lick it off." Harry felt the man grabbing tightly on the back of his neck. The pain was incredible. He thought for a moment like he might pass out.

What the hell was happening? What right did these two strangers have to maltreat him and threaten him?

Carlos said, "Sit still, old man, and let Maria clean up your stinking mess like she always does." Then he said to the nurse's aide, "Come on over here, baby. Harry here has made another special treat for you."

"Just shut up, Carlos. You disgust me," Maria said as she approached with her cleaning supplies. "Hey Ray, make sure you secure him before I start. You know he can be a fighter."

With that, the orderlies each took one of Harry's arms and strapped them to the chair, while Maria began to remove his pajama bottoms to begin a ritual she had done many times before and which she always found revolting. Harry wanted to close his eyes in confusion, shame, and humiliation. How had this happened to him? He started to struggle against his restraints and felt a sudden sharp pinching sensation in his right arm. Then the world began to fade away.

///

Harry opened his eyes to find himself back in his recliner, in his family room. He looked down at his hands and saw they weren't the hands of some older man but were back to normal.

"Wow! I must have had some sort of freaky nightmare."

One minute he had been paying his bills, watching a story about elder abuse, and then the next, he was . . . he was where? He couldn't recall all the details. He looked down and saw that none of the items he used to pay his bills were nearby; no checkbook, no bank statements, no envelopes, no stamps, nothing. But he was sure he had just been paying his bills. He closed his eyes in frustration.

///

"You don't understand what's happening, do you, Dad?" A voice said from somewhere across the room. Harry opened his eyes and again saw the shriveled hands of an older man resting on his pajamas. He was lying in what looked like a hospital bed; his head elevated to almost a sitting position.

He looked in the direction of the voice and saw a face that seemed vaguely familiar yet not recognizable. The man appeared to be in his late thirties, with a severely receding hairline, a brown mustache, and glasses. The man had called him Dad, but that wasn't possible. He and Eva only had one son, Brad, and he was only nineteen. This man was decades older than Brad.

"Who, who are you? What do you want from me?" Harry asked, bewildered.

The man stood and walked toward the bed. "I know you don't recognize me, Dad; you never do. I come to visit you every weekend, and we go through this same ritual week after week. Dad, it's me, your son. It's Brad."

"Nonsense! You're not my son. My Brad is only nineteen years old. You've got to be almost forty."

"I'm thirty-nine, Dad, and you're eighty-three. You have some problems with remembering. It has to do with . . . well, with your Alzheimer's."

"Alzheimer's? Don't be ridiculous! Look, young man. I don't know who you are or who you think you are, but you're not my son. I'm not eighty-three. And I certainly don't have Alzheimer's disease. Where my wife, she'll straighten this out, you'll see. Eva? Where are you, Eva?" Harry's voice grew louder, and his face reddened as he became more agitated. A sheen of sweat formed on his bald, spotted head. Brad knew the signs, and this wasn't good.

"Please, Dad, don't get so worked up. Take it easy. The doctor says your heart isn't well. Please, Dad."

But Harry was having none of it. He shouted even louder, "Eva? Where are you, Eva? I know you're nearby somewhere."

"Please, Dad, don't. Mom's not here; she can't hear you." Then after a hesitation, he said with frustration, "Mom's dead, Dad. Your wife, my mother, died over ten years ago. Don't you remember, Dad? Can't you understand? God, I hate this damned disease!"

Now Harry was angrier than ever. He shouted, "Liar! Liar, I tell you! I don't know who you are or what this place is, but I'm getting out of here and going home. I'm going to be with my precious Eva." Harry started to get up from the bed then slumped back down, clutching his chest again the tremendous pressure and pain he was experiencing.

///

Harry awoke in his recliner as sunlight streamed in through the French doors leading to his patio. Across the room, his television played a repeat of a *CBS Sunday Morning* program about elder abuse in retirement homes. On his lap was his checkbook. To his right was a stack of envelopes from a variety of companies and a bank statement. It was time to pay the bills and balance the checkbook. Harry breathed a sigh of relief. He must have fallen asleep again and had another nightmare.

"How's bill-paying going?" A pleasant voice said from behind him as his wife Eva walked into the family room.

"Eva, thank goodness you're here."

"Of course, I'm here, Harry. I was just upstairs getting a shower, remember?"

Harry hesitated then said, "Yes. I remember. It's just that I must have fallen back to sleep and had a bad nightmare. I can't remember what it was about, but I have a feeling that you were gone in my dream, and it was horrible not being with you."

"Not to worry, Sweetie. I'm here, and you're here with me now, and neither of us will ever be apart again."

THE GOLDEN ANKH

"Cursed is the man who dies, but the evil done by him survives."
—ABU BAKR

"Cursed be he above all others who's enslaved by love of money.
Money takes the place of brothers. Money takes the place of
parents. Money brings us war and slaughter."
—ANACREON

The man known only as Mr. Smith stood next to his car along the sand-blown road far outside the town known as Dahshur, south of Cairo. The full moon rose high above the desert as the calm winds blew sand against Smith's kerchief-covered face. He was halfway between the Pyramid of Dahshur and what was known as the Bent Pyramid.

In the distance, he could see a dim single headlight approaching. He knew this would be Kadir. He recognized the familiar sound of Kadir's beat-to-death 2013 Peugeot Vivacity 125. Smith had met the Egyptian here many times before.

The scooter stopped about twenty feet away from Smith as Kadir got off and shook the sand from his brown and striped kaftan, resembling a dog shaking off after coming in from a rainstorm. Kadir lifted his goggles from his eyes and unwrapped his keffiyeh, revealing his skull cap and long, tangled beard.

Smith noticed the man didn't wear his usual sly grin, complete with most of his teeth missing, but looked not only severe but under great stress.

"Good to see you, Kadir. I was eager to see what you have for me this evening. I hope all is well. You seem a bit agitated."

"I am, Mr. Smith," the man said in his heavily accented English, "It is because of what I have brought to sell you. I would appreciate it if we could get our business over with quickly, and I can be on my way."

Kadir kept turning to look around him as if suspecting someone might suddenly arrive. His right hand nervously gripped at the pocket where Smith knew Kadir kept his blade.

Suddenly feeling a bit uncomfortable himself, Smith asked, "Are you sure you're ok Kadir. If not, perhaps we should postpone this for some other day."

"No! No, I say," Kadir said with perhaps too much insistence. "It is imperative that we complete this transaction immediately."

Smith agreed, "Very well then, Kadir. What do you have for me?"

Kadir looked around again to make sure no one was watching him.

"Kadir? What the hell's going on? We're in the middle of the desert here. There's nobody around to bother us. So how about you relax."

"I'm so sorry, Mr. Smith. I'm not quite myself this evening. However, I do have something extraordinary, as you will soon see."

"What is it, Kadir?"

"It is an ankh, Mr. Smith."

"An ankh, you say? You're brought me dozens of ankhs over the years. There's nothing special about a bloody ankh Kadir."

"But this one certainly is special. It is a golden ankh," the Egyptian said while still looking about cautiously.

"A golden ankh, is it? What sort of fool do you take me for Kadir? I can go on any of a dozen websites and buy a so-called 'golden ankh' for a few dollars. Granted, it will be gold-plated tin from China. Sorry, Kadir, but you know I have no time for worthless trinkets."

"But Mr. Smith, I assure you this is no trinket. This golden ankh is genuine, recovered two days ago from an ancient tomb."

Now Kadir had Smith's attention. He asked, "Which tomb Kadir? Which site was it?"

"Sorry, Mr. Smith. It would be better for you if you didn't know. There were, shall we say, extenuating circumstances involved in its recovery, hence the reason for my desire for a quick transaction."

"Very well, Kadir. Then please just show me the piece."

Kadir pulled an item from one of his left pockets. It was wrapped in a dirty scrap of cloth and bound with twine. Kadir laid the bundle on the hood of Smith's car and untied it. As soon as Smith saw the gorgeous medallion in the moonlight, its dull and pitted golden surface glowing eerily, he knew this was no novelty story bobble but was the real deal. He recognized the familiar cross shape with the elliptical top. The form always reminded Smith of a person standing with their arms extended outward and their legs pressed tightly together. He knew such an artifact would bring millions from the right collector.

"You stole this, Kadir," Smith said not as a question but a statement.

"Yes, Mr. Smith, I did. However, this should not come as any great surprise to you since we both know everything I've ever sold to you in the past was procured by, shall we say, less than legitimate means."

"Now wait right there, Kadir. I've always asked you whether or not you've come by your treasures honestly, and you always said you had."

"This is true, but only because we both knew that was what you needed to hear. However, we both also understood the unspoken truth. Don't bother denying it either, Mr. Smith. In the case of this golden ankh, I, unfortunately, do not have the time or energy to continue with this ruse. Sadly, I had to pay much too high a price for my troubles. Because of that, this will have to be our last transaction. That is why I need to insist on the payment of one hundred thousand dollars American."

"A hundred thousand? Are you out of your mind, Kadir!" Smith argued, even though the ankh would be a bargain at twice that price. Kadir's evident agitation told Smith that the Egyptian would take whatever price he offered. Smith believed he knew what Kadir had done to get the ankh and why he needed so much money so fast.

Smith said, "Did you kill someone to get this ankh, Kadir?"

The man hesitated for a moment, then said quietly, "Yes, Mr. Smith, I did. I had to kill two guards to get this for you. That is why I need to have the money and right away. I must flee the country immediately. I have arranged for safe passage out of Egypt, but it will cost me dearly. If no one has yet found the bodies, someone likely will by morning. Then the American scientists at the dig will find the golden ankh missing. When they see I have not reported for work, they will figure things out and send the authorities to come for me. My window of escape is a narrow one."

Smith noticed the man absently touching the bulge in his right pocket made by the handle of his knife. He assumed this was the same knife Kadir had used to slay the two guards.

"I'm sorry, Kadir. But this ankh is too hot. It'll have too much attention on it, making it impossible for me to move. You should never have taken such drastic action."

"Please, Mr. Smith. My life here in Egypt is over. If I don't escape, I will be a dead man. What if you we're to pay me seventy-five thousand dollars now and twenty-five more after you have sold the treasure. Surely a man of your wealth could afford to hide the ankh and wait for things to, as you say, cool down."

"Here's what I'm going to do, Kadir. I'll pay you fifty thousand in cash for the ankh; right now, tonight. But that's all I will pay, and the only reason is that I'm feeling generous. It'll be enough money to get you safely out of Egypt and will set you up for a time in your new place of residence, wherever that might be."

"But Mr. Smith. That, that is thievery! The value of this ankh is, well, it is priceless. After all the business we've done in the past, how can you dare to cheat me so?"

"Poor Kadir. You simply don't understand business. And I don't have the patience to try to explain things to you. Fifty thousand is my final offer. Take it or leave it."

Smith knew he had Kadir right where he wanted him. There was simply no way he could refuse. He waved a dismissive hand and the Egyptian and slid the cloth holding the ankh toward Kadir.

"If that's the way you want to play this Kadir, then good luck finding another buyer. I suspect you probably could eventually, that is if you aren't either rotting in an Egyptian prison or dead."

"Fine, fine," Kadir said with frustration, realizing he should never have let Smith know of his troubles. "Fifty thousand will have to do."

"Excellent, Kadir," Smith replied as he turned and reached into the back seat of his sedan to retrieve the money from his briefcase. Kadir had seen the man do this many times before and knew he probably had at least a hundred thousand cash in the suitcase, if not more.

As Smith turned his back to get the money, Kadir picked up the ankh with his left hand and withdrew the curved blade with his right, gripping the handle tightly. He would get the money he deserved and more. He would leave Smith's body to rot in the desert and steal his car in the process. The authorities would find Smith and the accursed ankh. All he cared about was getting his money and getting away. He raised his knife hand in preparation for his strike when Smith turned, pointing a pistol equipped with a silencer directly at this chest.

"I've decided fifty thousand is too much, Kadir."

Before the Egyptian had a chance to react, Smith pumped three slugs directly into his chest. Kadir fell onto his back, dead before he hit the ground. The hand holding the golden ankh fell across his chest, landing in the puddle of still-warm blood that had collected there. Smith looked down at the corpse in the moonlight. Then something strange happened.

The golden ankh began to glow brightly with a rhythmic pulse, radiating brighter with each beat. Soon it was so effervescent, Smith had to shield his eyes, feeling like he might go blind if he didn't protect them. The radiance began to die down, and Smith could again see the golden ankh lying on Kadir's chest. Then he realized the symbol was no longer on top of the corpse but sank into the dead man's crimson wound. In his mind, Smith imagined millions of dollars disappearing along with it. He wasn't about to let that happen.

Smith saw the Egyptian's knife lying next to his body. He bent down to retrieve it. Smith wasn't thrilled with the idea of cutting the ankh from the man's body, but nothing would prevent him from possessing it. He picked up the blade and stood for a moment staring at the corpse, steeling himself for the gruesome task awaiting him. That was when he saw Kadir's left foot twitch.

"Just an involuntary reaction," Smith said with more confidence than he felt. "A muscular reflex, nothing more." That was when Kadir's arm jerked, and his eyes opened, shining with the same eerie golden glow as had come from the ankh itself.

Then impossibly, the dead man began to get to his feet clumsily. Panicking, Smith threw the blade at the resurrected creature before him. Not being skilled at knife throwing, Smith assumed the knife would simply strike and bounce off Kadir. He was shocked to see the knife sink itself hilt-deep into the dead man's throat. Yet the undead thing stood unfazed by the attack. The creature raised its arms and began advancing toward Smith.

He withdrew his pistol and pumped the remaining bullets into the walking corpse. The Kadir creature continued to advance as Smith tried to back further away. That was when Smith's heel caught on some debris on the highway, and he fell backward, striking his head on the road surface.

He lay in the sand, trying desperately to remain conscious but fading in and out of the blackness. As he tried to focus, his cloudy vision caught flashing images of someone coming ever closer. His brain felt as foggy as his vision. He believed there was some reason he should be afraid, but he couldn't recall why.

He sensed someone crawling on top of him and could make out the Egyptian's dirty face coming ever closer. He saw the creature opening its mouth wide, revealing a graveyard of scattered rotted tombstone teeth. Before he could do anything to resist, he felt searing pain as the wretched creature tore his throat out and the warmth of his lifeblood soaked into his shirt. Then the blackness returned with a vengeance, and this time it remained.

LEGS

How many legs does a dog have if you call his tail a leg? Four.
Saying that a tail is a leg doesn't make it a leg.
—ABRAHAM LINCOLN

Darling, the legs aren't so beautiful; I just know
what to do with them.
—MARLENE DIETRICH

When you have got an elephant by the hind legs, and he is trying
to run away, it's best to let him run.
—ABRAHAM LINCOLN

She's got legs. She knows how to use them.
—ZZ TOP

The gray Toyota RAV4 slowly made its way along the foggy two-lane, its headlights scarcely capturing the recently harvested cornfields along the roadside. Short, broken stalks could rose from the frozen ground, their tattered tips scraping along the bottom of the fog bank. In the distance, the florescent orange netting of the recently installed snow fence was barely visible as the mist weaved its way between the plastic webbing encompassing it like a shroud.

"Man, this fog is thick," Allen Carpenter said to his wife Deidra, who was staring out the side window, mesmerized like a child in a candy shop.

"It's so surreal out there. I can sense the mystery in the fog. It's like a magical fantasy landscape, something not of this world."

Allen loved his wife desperately, but she always seemed to live on a plane separate from reality. She was what some people referred to as sensitive. He tolerated all of her new age crystal mumbo jumbo and talk of her clairvoyance and mysticism because . . . well, because he just loved her.

"It is weird looking out there. But my real concern when it gets this foggy is watching out for deer crossing the highway. I mean, we just bought this new car two weeks ago, and I don't want Bambi's mom or dad walking out in front of us and totaling it."

Deidra said, "I'm not sensing anything large out there in the fog, at least not at the moment."

"Well, that's good to hear, sweetie. I feel much better now." Allen always humored his wife when she was in mystic mode, as he liked to call it. He was at least a lot more tolerant of her beliefs than some of his friends were.

He recalled when he introduced her to one of his buddies from work, Bob Jackson, a big man tipping the scales at about two-sixty. After the introduction, Deidra had said, "Good to meet you. I'm Deidra; I'm a medium."

Bob had looked at Allen for a moment in confusion, and then being the proverbial office jokester, said, "Hi. I'm Bob. I'm an extra-large."

The joke went right over Deidra's head, a fact for which Allen had been grateful. But that was just how she was. She had little sense of humor and always seemed to be off somewhere other than the real world.

Suddenly Allen hit the brakes, pulled his car over to the side of the road, and pressed the button for the four-way emergency flashers saying, "What's that up ahead? It looks like a large dog walking out of the cornfield, or maybe it's a fawn. I can't tell because of the stupid fog. What do you think?"

Deidra said nothing. She just stared at the spot Allen had indicated. Four long spindly legs could be seen at the side of the road, seeming to poke down out of the thick fogbank. They appeared to be uncertain, like a newborn trying to walk for the first time.

"Hey, isn't there a dairy farm is around here somewhere? You don't think one of the calves somehow got out of the barn, do you?"

Deidra sat silent for a moment, then said in a hypnotic-sounding voice, "It's . . . not . . . a calf."

"Well, I can see it's not a dog either, so it must be a fawn. Look how strangely it's walking, like it's disoriented or something. Hey, maybe it was hit by a car, someone that traveled here before us. I'd better see if it's alright," Allen said as he opened his door and unbuckled his seat belt.

"Don't Allen. Don't go. Something isn't right. I can feel it," Deidra pleaded.

"Well, I can see something's not right, Honey. That animal is hurt. Maybe there's something I can do to help it."

"But something's very wrong, Allen. I don't think this is what you think it is."

Allen said with a sigh, "Look, Sweetie. I trust your judgment, but I have to do something. I have to make sure this animal is ok." Then before Deidra could reply, Allen shut the door and walked around the front of the vehicle, the headlights illuminating him as the fog began to encircle him. Soon only his lower torso and legs were visible.

As Allen got closer to the animal, something unimaginable happened; the four legs went vertically up into the fog, disappearing from the roadway altogether. Deidra gaped slack-jawed as every muscle in her body began to tense. It was as if something had lifted the small creature upward. A moment later, she heard Allen scream.

The cry was unearthly, one of pure terror and agony. She saw Allen's legs leaving the roadway as he, too, was being lifted upward. She cursed herself for her sensitivity as she could feel Allen's terror and experience his pain as something squeezed him in a vice-like grip, forcing the air from his lungs and crushing his ribs. She could hear his bones cracking in her mind as something reduced her husband's body to nothing more than a sack of broken, fragmented bones and fluids. Then all sense of Allen's existence was gone.

A moment later, the animal's legs dropped down from the fog. They came to rest once again on the side of the road. The mist was still too dense to make out anything but the creature's four legs. It seemed as if the legs were coercing Deidra to come out of the car as Allen had done.

She sat in the car crying for the loss of her husband but was too much in shock to figure out what she might do next. The four legs just stood wobbling by the side of the road. Then to Deidra's surprise, the fog began to lift rapidly. It was extraordinary to see as it rose upward like the curtain of a theater. She stared at the four legs expecting to see the creature's head any second, but instead, she saw what looked like a hand leading to an enormous wrist, then an arm as the fog continued to dissipate.

She sat back deep in her seat, wishing the upholstery would surround her like a shield and protect her from the horror she was seeing. In a matter of seconds, the fog was gone. Standing in the road ahead of her was a massive creature more than fifty feet tall. The things Allen had mistaken for legs were four fingers on the end of a long, brown, muscular arm glistening with sweat.

Following the arm upward, Deidra saw the creature's hideous face. Its head was massive with large bulging red-rimmed yellow cat-like eyes. The creature's nose was more of a hog snout than a nose, and it had thick red lips with dozens of tusk-like fangs jutting out from glimmering ruby gums. Between two of the yellowed blood-smeared teeth, she saw remnants of her husband's leg attached to one of his sneakers. She recalled how she had just bought him those sneakers for his birthday.

Still in shock, she couldn't understand how what she thought of as her powers had failed her. She had known something was wrong about those four legs in the fog, but she hadn't expected them to be what they had been; a decoy, a lure, a trap to ensnare her beloved husband. And now he was gone, devoured by this monster.

But how could this be? What sort of demon was this, and from where had it come? She couldn't wrap her mind around what was happening. Before she realized it, the massive beast reached down and grabbed the roof of her SUV from both sides. Its fingers shattered the glass showering her with broken window fragments. Just a few inches from her face, she could see the things she had mistaken for animal legs.

They were dark and covered with thick flesh, wisps of hair, and sweat. The smell coming from them was woodsy and stank of musk. The fingers tightened and crushed the roof as it separated from the SUV and pulled upward. The creature threw the metal far off into the cornfield and then turned to look at Deidra once more.

The beast's eyes widened in anticipation of its upcoming meal. Its nostrils flared with delight taking in her scent. A long tongue slid from its gaping maw and licked its lips. The remnants of Allen's leg fell from its lips, and the creature slapped it too out into the cornfield. Then it reached down to pick Deidra from the car and make her its next meal.

She closed her eyes, wishing the creature would vanish but knowing her violent death was just seconds away. But her death never came. The beast had stopped with its spindly fingers just a few inches from Deidra's face. She looked up and saw something in the monster's yellow eyes she had not expected. She saw anger and fear. The creature had seen something in her which caused it to recoil. It was her power.

In a last act of fury, the creature's massive foot came out of nowhere and kicked the side of the vehicle, causing it to flip end for end as it barrel-rolled out into the cornfield. Deidra was knocked unconscious, which was how she remained until she later awoke amid a barrage of flashing lights and the disjointed conversations of rescue personnel.

"Must . . . been flying . . ." One voice said.

"Roof . . . torn right off . . ." Another exclaimed.

"Lucky . . . not dead. . . ."

"Where's the driver. . . ."

"No sign . . ."

"Allen?" Deidra said in a raspy voice she barely recognized as her own, "Where's Allen."

"Ma'am, please. Don't try to talk. You're going to be ok, just take it easy, and everything's going to be alright."

"Allen. Where's my Allen?" She tried before blacking out once more.

"Who do you suppose Allen was, the driver?" One of the EMTs on the scene asked. "Could this Allen be her boyfriend?"

Another EMT looked down and saw a ring on her left hand. "Could be her husband, I suppose."

"Hey, I found something over here," a young policeman shouted from nearby. "And it's pretty disgusting."

"What is it, Johnson?" Another policeman inquired.

"It looks like the bottom half of a leg in a sneaker," he replied.

"Where's the rest of him?"

"I . . . I don't know. All I found was a leg." Then the young officer bent over and vomited.

The other policeman shook his head, puzzled, and said, "I just don't get it. Over the past six months, we've found almost a dozen abandoned and smashed cars along this stretch of road and not a body in sight. Now not only do we have a survivor, but we have a leg. I don't know what this means, but maybe this woman will be able to make sense of it all when she regains consciousness."

But they would never solve their mystery since the fantastic story Deidra would tell was way too far-fetched for anyone to believe. And once the police investigated and learned Deidra saw herself as having some sort of mystical powers, anything she said had no chance of being thought of as truth.

Then again, there was that leg. Its stump end did look as if something had chewed it. But that could have been nothing more than a tear from the severity of the accident. It had been capable of ripping the roof off of an SUV. But where was the rest of the husband? The incident would just go on the record as one more unexplained situation along that stretch of roadway on a foggy night, as would all the rest in the future. And there would be many more in the years to follow.

But Deidra knew what she had seen, and someday she would find a way to prove it or die trying. But for now, she sat quietly in her living room surrounded by her various mystical crystals and talismans, staring at the lone sneaker sitting on her fireplace mantle.

RELAX

"Deep into that darkness peering, long I stood there,
wondering, fearing, doubting, dreaming dreams no mortal
ever dared to dream before."
—Edgar Allen Poe

The knock came unexpectedly in the middle of the night. Rick half-opened his eyes, still in that strange fugue state between sleeping and awakening. As his eyes began to close, he once again heard the loud banging sound. This time his eyes opened wide as he became alert and aware the sound was coming from his front door.

He hated whenever his phone rang or someone came to his door late at night because chances were excellent that it had nothing to do with him. Such things often happened in his apartment building. Someone would be looking for someone else but getting the apartment number wrong. He also knew from experience the interruption would cause him to be awake for hours. He could already feel his heart pounding in his chest from the sudden awakening.

Still in a stupor, he shouted, "Relax. I'm coming; I'm coming already."

Then he threw open the door without first looking through the peephole. To his surprise, he saw his old friend, Todd, standing in the hallway. Todd stood silently, staring at him with a strange look in his eyes. At first, Rick was glad to see his friend standing there. That was until his mind cleared a bit, and he recalled how Todd had died more than two years earlier.

Rick took an involuntary step backward, unsure of what was happening. He quickly appraised his dead friend and suddenly understood what was so strange about him, besides the obvious fact, he was deceased. It was more than his cold, icy stare or even his dusky blue lips and chalky pallor. It was the piercing, almost angry look in those filmed-over eyes.

He didn't know why Todd would have any reason to be upset with him. Rick had never done his friend any wrong during his life and had nothing to do with contributing to Todd's death either. Todd had died suddenly of an aneurism at the age of thirty-five.

No one could have expected or predicted it, especially not Rick. The other thing Rick couldn't comprehend was why upon finding a long-term friend standing in his doorway, he hadn't screamed or turned and tried to flee. Indeed, he would have felt justified to take such action. Yet here he stood looking curiously at a . . . what? A ghost?

Suddenly the thing, which had once been Todd, took a step forward, all the while never taking his clouded eyes off Rick.

"No! No, Todd. You stay right where you are," Rick tried to say, but to his surprise, his voice came out several octaves lower than expected and had a slow and somewhat liquidy quality. It made Rick think of someone talking in super-slow motion underwater. That was when he noticed how the air around him had taken on a consistency, which felt thick and soupy.

The Todd creature seemed to be trying to speak as well, its wrinkled blue lips parting to reveal blackened and yellowed tombstone teeth. The mouth opened incredibly wide and began snapping like a crocodile's jaws. The thing reached out with its bony fingers and tried to grab hold of Rick.

Rick slowly turned with great effort and attempted to run away. He hoped perhaps if he could make it to his bedroom, he could lock himself inside and fashion some sort of weapon. At the very least, Rick could climb out onto the fire escape. However, He found his movements awkward and incredibly slow.

Feeling as if he was running in a vast sea filled with Jell-O, Rick recalled how he had once seen a slow-motion video on television of a bullet shot into a container of ballistic gelatin. His body now felt like that bullet, and the air around him had become the gelatin. Behind him, he could hear the creature getting ever closer. If he could only make it to the bedroom, he would be fine. However, even as the thought entered his mind, the door to the room slowly closed, blocking his entry.

Rick looked to his left and saw his living room window standing open. He struggled against the thick tide of gelatinous air to get to the window. His second-floor apartment only had access to the fire escape through his bedroom. He believed he could survive the drop to the ground below with minimal injury. Whatever damage he might suffer had to be better than the fate he imagined was waiting behind him.

Disregarding his original plan for a hanging drop, Rick chose to dive toward the open window for reasons he couldn't explain. He had the sensation of swimming underwater as his body propelled through the gelatmosphere and out the window.

He braced himself for the impact against the ground below and the pain which would follow. However, the collision never came. He discovered he was still soaring forward and was doing so at an ever-increasing rate. That was when he saw the side of a brick building coming rapidly toward him.

Rick braced himself once again for impact, sensing this would be much worse than a two-story fall. To his surprise, as his body hit the bricks painlessly, it instantly morphed into a semi-liquified version of his original self, spreading out in a spherical mass of undulating flesh.

The Rick-blob puddled along the side of the building for a moment. Then it began to flow down to the alley below. When it reached the ground, the mass slowly reshaped itself once again into the form of Rick. This unexpected occurrence was even more disturbing than initially finding his dead friend knocking at his apartment door.

He looked around him, expecting to see his street or at least something that looked familiar, but there was nothing he recognized. He wasn't even in the city any longer. Rick was shocked to discover he was standing in the middle of a cemetery somewhere out in the country. It was still the middle of the night, but the full moon shone brightly in the clear sky above.

The cemetery appeared abandoned, its many headstones vandalized and pushed over. Some had been spray painted with graffiti. Rick could see gnarled, near-dead trees leaning at bizarre and twisted angles standing guard over the graves like sentries for the dead in the moonlight.

The grass and weeds had grown very high due to neglect. Rick wondered what sort of place this was and why he was here. Walking about aimlessly, he came upon a large stone. It wasn't damaged like the others and stood perfectly straight. The burial mound in front of the tombstone indicated signs of a recent interment. He couldn't understand why there would be a fresh burial in such a decrepit, unkempt graveyard. None of this made any sense to him.

Rick walked around to the front of the stone, stood on the soft burial mound to read the inscription. There were no names or dates carved on the polished, glossy surface of the stone. It was blank save for a single closed eyeball etched into its shiny marble surface. He stood and stared at the image for a few seconds, sure that based on all the bizarre events, which had already happened to him so far, the thing would pop open and frighten him into a coronary. But fortunately, it remained closed. He started to turn to walk away but never got to complete his turn.

Two hands shot up from the dirt and grabbed tightly onto Rick's ankles. He looked down in horror and saw the hideous appendages. The flesh was gray and rotten, sloughing off in places revealing the pale, white bone beneath. Worms and maggots crawled in and out of the decomposing skin. Rick could smell an ungodly stench arising from the ground below him. The skeletal hands pulled his legs down deeper into the ground. He looked back at the gravestone and saw the carved eye now wide open and staring angrily at him, just as dead Todd had done.

Struggling futilely against the vice-like grip, Rick thrashed and tried to scream as he sunk chest-deep in the soft soil, but he found he couldn't produce a sound. Not that it would have mattered anyway since no one was around the abandoned cemetery to hear him. Soon the dirt was pressing against the bottom of his chin. Although he lifted his head as far as possible, the earth passed rapidly over his bottom lip and into his mouth. Rick closed his lips tightly together, but the dirt soon filled his nostrils. His heart slammed so hard against his chest he was sure it was preparing to explode. Then as he closed his eyes in the final acceptance of his fate, he felt the cold soil covering his head.

Rick opened his eyes with a start, hoping the nightmare he was experiencing was finally over. He noticed he was standing in the hallway of an apartment building, his apartment building. Rick stood directly in front of his front door. He tried the handle and found the door locked. Rick knocked on the door. He had no idea why he did so, as no one could be inside since he was standing outside. He just felt he had to knock.

There was no response, so he knocked again, harder this time.

He heard an angry voice which sounded surprisingly like his own shouting, "Relax. I'm coming. I'm coming already."

IMAGE IS EVERYTHING

He awoke in a strange place with an ungodly throbbing in his skull. An icy chill enveloped his entire body, the result of the dampness of the room. Stone walls, glistening with moisture, surrounded him. There were no windows and pale light from a single naked bulb suspended from a frayed wire, high above him.

He sat up quickly, discovering he had been lying on a thin, damp mattress atop a skeletal metal frame. It rattled as he threw his legs over the side and attempted to stand. When he did, the top of his head felt like it was about to explode. A wave of dizziness overtook him, and he feared he might collapse. He braced himself against the wet wall and waited for the feeling of vertigo to pass. He fought the rising need to vomit.

Glancing about the room, he judged it to be not much bigger than a good-sized closet. He saw no sink or toilet, just a metal bucket in the corner of the room. He supposed at least that was a good thing. If the desire to toss his cookies didn't subside, at least he wouldn't have to puke on the floor. After a few seconds, the nauseous feeling blessedly started to go away. If only he could do something about his pounding skull.

Looking past the foot of his narrow bed, he saw a tall metal door with a slot in the bottom about three inches high and eighteen inches wide. He had seen spaces like this in movies and knew they were a way to pass food into a jail cell. There was a small, barred opening at the top of the door.

"David F. Lawrence," A disembodied voice suddenly called to him, sounding as if it were coming from a tinny loudspeaker. He looked around his cell and couldn't find the source. Perhaps it was located in the hall outside the door. The voice sounded distorted as if filtered through some electronic voice-altering device.

D. F. Lawrence was his pen name, the one he used when writing his crime novels. His real name was Larry Davidson. However, Larry understood the value of using a name similar to the famous author D. H. Lawrence and how it might help promote brand recognition. In his world of constant promotion, he knew that image was considered everything. That meant it was possible whoever was holding him captive might only know him by his nom de plume. At least Larry hoped his captor didn't know more than that about him. Because if he knew about his real name, his wife, and his family, that could be a real game-changer.

"Answer me now, please," the mysterious voice requested almost mechanically, "You are D. F. Lawrence, are you not?"

Larry was both angry and uneasy at the same time. He had no idea why someone had brought him to this place or how, and the pain in his head was so severe it made him feel like crying.

"Why, why am I here? Who are you? What's the meaning of this?"

"Meaning, you ask?" The voice replied, "The meaning is quite simple, Mr. Lawrence. I've drugged and kidnapped you, and I'm holding you for ransom."

"Ransom? Why do you think anyone would or could pay any ransom for me? I'm no one special. I have no money."

"But you are D. F. Lawrence, the mystery and crime novelist. Correct?"

Larry hesitated for a moment, wondering if it might be better if he lied and denied who he was. Then he realized if this lunatic went to the trouble of drugging and kidnapping him, he already knew who he was. He reluctantly replied, "Um, yes, I am D. F. Lawrence, but I still don't understand . . ."

The voice interrupted, "You have published more than twenty novels and seven short story collections over the past fifteen years.

Your short stories have also appeared in more than one hundred multi-author anthologies as well. Is that not also correct?"

"Yes, but . . ."

"You obviously must have made a lot of money from the sale of all those books."

Larry suddenly understood this kidnapper had fallen for the same uniformed illusion all non-writers had. The general public had the predisposed idea that you instantly became rich and famous when publishing a book. Sadly, Larry knew the realities of the world of publishing, which few outsiders could ever hope to understand.

"No. Look, I'm sorry. There's been a terrible mistake. It appears you're misinformed. I am indeed a D. F Lawrence. And although I do love writing, it's a hobby for me and nothing more. I only write on a part-time basis. You see, I have a day job. That's what pays my bills, not writing."

The modified voice replied, "Don't play games with me, Mr. Lawrence. Do you or do you not collect royalties for your work?"

"Uh, well, yes. Yes, I do, but I'm ashamed to admit I hardly make any money whatsoever from my book royalties."

The mysterious voice suddenly took on a more menacing quality, "Do you seriously expect me to believe such a ridiculous tale? Do you take me for a fool? I've seen your books advertised on websites from all around the world. They are in paperback, hardcover, and digital formats. Surely you must be collecting a fortune in royalties."

"No. Please just listen to me. I swear that's not true," Larry pleaded in frustration, "Last year, I made less than sixty dollars in royalties. Does that sound like a fortune to you?"

"Don't lie to me, Mr. Lawrence. You have a publisher. You have professional representation. Perhaps your publisher should be the one who pays for your release."

Becoming more frustrated by the minute, Larry tried again to explain, "I honestly wish that were true, but it's not. My publisher is a small-time operation as well. He, too, works at a full-time job and only runs the business as a side project. Please, just let me go. I haven't seen you so I can't identify you. I swear there's no one to pay my ransom."

Still, the voice insisted, "Do you honestly think I'm going to fall for that story, Mr. Lawrence. I've seen your website; it gives the impression that you're a world-renowned award-winning author. The same is true of your publisher. His site projects the image of a large first-rate publishing house."

"Don't you get it? That's because they're supposed to. See, in our business, image is everything. If we ever hope to make the major leagues, we have to put that sort of impression out there. We have to make people believe we are the real deal, so someday we actually can be the real deal. Didn't you ever hear the expression 'fake it 'til you make it?'"

There was a brief hesitation, then the voice replied in a way that sent chills racing down Larry's spine, "But I've seen your home as well. You must be selling a ton of books to afford such a nice home."

Larry still hoped he might be able to talk his way out of this situation. However, he was now more concerned than ever. Larry just realized his worst fears. He now had to worry about his wife and kids. This psycho had seen his house and knew where Larry lived. He could get to Larry's family if he chose to. Larry decided to try to keep the maniac talking. Maybe he could figure some way out of this mess. But to do so, he'd have to stay alive.

He tried yet again to explain, "Look, I'm an accountant. Ok? I know that may not seem like a very glamorous career choice, but it's that boring career that pays for my house. I'm not some world-renowned author. If I had to rely on my writing income, I couldn't rent the basement of an outhouse."

The voice said, "Do you seriously think I'm that stupid, Mr. Lawrence. I know royalties aren't the only potential source of income for writers. There are book shows, personal appearances, book signing events, and speaking engagements. You have numerous social media accounts where you promote your books. Each one has several thousand followers. They likely buy books directly from you for cash. That's a potential for thousands of book sales. And my guess is you fail to report all of these cash sales to the government. As you can see, Mr. Lawrence, I've done my homework."

"Please, please just listen to me. I'm telling you, it's all an illusion. It's all just part trying to get my name out there so maybe someday I might have a chance at being as rich and famous as people believe I already am."

Finally, Larry couldn't take it any longer. His shouts echoed in his empty cell, "Don't you get it? Just because I have thousands of followers on social media, it doesn't mean a thing! Social media doesn't produce sales at all. It's just a place for people to broadcast their thoughts. If it weren't free, I wouldn't even bother going on social media. I only use it to try to promote my writing, even though it does nothing. Social media is like the Wild West! It's uncontrollable and unpredictable. It's just a bastion of lunacy! I once read somewhere that being popular on social media is like sitting at the 'cool table' in an insane asylum."

"What, what did you just say?"

"I said . . . never mind; it was nothing, just a dumb joke. Forget it."

The voice over the speakers sounded extremely angry now, "So do you think making jokes about mental illness is appropriate, Mr. Lawrence? Do you find the subject humorous?"

Larry realized his mistake. He should have considered how someone had to be more than a trifle off-balance to kidnap him and put him in a dungeon. Hadn't he even just been thinking of his captor as a lunatic or a maniac moments earlier?

"You think all of this is something to joke about, don't you, Mr. Lawrence? If you've never spent time in one of those horrible places, you have no right to ridicule those of us who have."

"Great," Larry thought to himself, "This guy really was in a nuthouse, and I just managed to push some buttons I shouldn't have pushed."

"Those places can be a hell on earth for people like me. They often cause more harm than good. And you, Mr. high-and-mighty world-famous author, think you have the right to judge me? Does that make you feel better? Does that help support your fragile artistic ego?"

Larry stammered, "N . . . n . . . no. Not at all. You don't understand."

"I don't understand? It's you who don't understand, Mr. Lawrence. Or should I call you Larry, Larry Davidson?"

Larry felt a sickening feeling rise inside him.

"That's right, Larry. I know all about you and your family. I know a lot about you. You see, in your eyes, I may be crazy, but I think you just discovered I'm not stupid. I will admit, however, I did make one mistake regarding your financial value. I made the same misassumptions a lot of people make. It appears your idea of the image being everything has worked quite well since you are all image and nothing else. Well, I guess that means you're no longer of any value to me as a potential source of revenue. But perhaps after your body is discovered in a few weeks, after I call in an anonymous tip, your family will benefit from whatever life insurance policy you may have. When that day comes, I'll be paying a visit to your lovely wife and children, and I'll collect from them what you were unable to provide me."

"You, you bastard," Larry shouted. "You can't do this. You can't get away with this."

"Well, Larry. Not only can I get away with it, but I already have. Goodbye, Larry."

With that, the light in Larry's cell went out, and darkness engulfed him. After several hours of screaming himself hoarse, Larry realized his captor had left him to die. He sat down on his damp mattress, listening to the metallic creaking of the springs, and wept.

WORMS

"Worms!" John Alexander shouted as he brought the point of his spade down on the squirming creature cleaving it neatly in two wriggling halves. Then he turned the spade with the flat bottom facing down and began to smash at the soil shouting angrily with each subsequent thrust. "I . . . hate . . . these stinking . . . slithering . . . dirt-crawling . . . things."

By the time he stopped, the two formerly twitching earthworm halves were gone from sight, likely still gyrating somewhere under the soil. John needed to get this work done before the next rainfall. If not, he knew what would happen then. There would be more of them, dozens, perhaps hundreds of the dreadful creatures crawling and slithering about his walk and driveway. He should have known better. He should have realized this before he built his home here. If so, he never would have done so. What the hell had he been thinking?

The land beneath John Alexander's subdivision was originally quite fertile. It was some of the richest farmland in Western Berks County, Pennsylvania. Although several feet of the fertile topsoil had been scraped off and resold by the developer, there was still about six inches of good earth resting atop a base of unforgiving clay.

One of the things John discovered rather quickly and found disturbing was the abundance of earthworms in the thin layer of dirt. Even though John understood the essential role worms played in aerating the soil and keeping it healthy, it did little to assuage his feelings. He hated the wretched creatures; he had always hated them his entire life. In John's mind, the only thing more revolting than the slimy things burrowing underground was the thought of the same disgusting critters were crawling over his flesh.

Some might consider his semi-phobia irrational; however, John didn't. When he was a child, he often recalled the older boys telling stories about how when you died, the worms came to feast on your body as it moldered in the grave. They even made up disgusting songs and rhymes about it chanting, "The worms crawl in, the worms crawl out, the green saliva comes out of your mouth." It didn't matter to John that the worms in these childhood poems were larvae and maggots. In his young mind, earthworms, larvae, or inchworms were all the same. He hated them all.

He often had nightmares of being buried and trapped naked inside a rotting wooden coffin, stinking of moisture, mold, and decay. He recalled how real everything seemed in these dreams as the cold, slime-covered creatures slinked over his exposed flesh. He always woke up at the same point in the nightmare, covered in sweat and panting like a dog after a long run. That was when the worms began to crawl over his lips, into his mouth, and slide down his throat.

As an adult, John found himself still plagued not only by dreaded thoughts of the horrible slimy things, but he now lived in a house surrounded by soil that was teaming with them. He learned this unfortunate bit of information following the first prolonged, heavy rainfall. That morning, while walking out to his car John noticed a particularly odd fishy odor. He looked down, and to his shock, John discovered his driveway covered with dozens of disgusting earthworms of all shapes and sizes. At first, he stood staring down at the horrible sight. Some were short and fat. Others long stretched out to nearly seven inches; all disgusting, all wriggling.

He considered getting his garden hose and blasting his driveway clean but realized the disgusting things would puddle at the bottom of the driveway, and that might be even more disgusting. John learned the best way to get to the safety of his car was to tiptoe carefully between the squirming creatures. He succeeded in doing so, scarcely managing to keep his breakfast in his stomach in the process. At one point, John stepped on an exceptionally thick and juicy critter, feeling it squish beneath his shoe. As he got his car door, open John scrapped his shoe on a bare spot in the driveway, eager to get the remains free of his sole.

As he drove through his neighborhood, John noticed every street and every driveway was in the same repulsive condition as his own. He felt as if the fishy stench was stuck in his sinuses and might linger there all day. His car rolled over worm after worm. He could only imagine what his tires and wheel wells must look like with dozens of wiggling half-dead worm carcasses dangling from them. The thought made his stomach lurch. He stopped at a twenty-four-hour automatic car wash on his way to work. He hated to spend the money, but he had no intention of either looking at the mess on his tires or washing the creatures off by himself.

That particular event had taken place several weeks earlier, and to his pleasure, after that, it had been a dry spring. As such, a similar heavy rain had not occurred since. However, he made up his mind by the time the next heavy rain came, his driveway would be worm-free. There was little he could do about the rest of his neighborhood or its streets, but at least he could try to stop the problem at his own home.

John began researching the elimination of earthworms from his lawn and found quite an abundance of helpful information. He learned that simply adding a bird feeder to his front yard might attract robins and other birds to eat the worms. He wasn't sure he wanted to go that route, however, as the thought of dozens of birds crapping all over his car was not much more appealing than the worms themselves.

He read that worms thrive in moist soil. If he didn't water his lawn, the number of worms might diminish. But his yard was still relatively new, and he didn't want to have to pay to have it reseeded if it dried out and the grass died. He also learned about pesticides and "chemical vermifuges," such as potassium permanganate and formalin. John felt as though he was reading in some foreign language, which he supposed he was. He also wasn't crazy about these chemicals since the literature said they didn't kill the worms but brought them out of the soil so he could sweep them away. The idea of his sweeping hundreds of worms down his driveway was more disgusting than stepping over them or using the hose on them.

When he was about to give up, John found some pesticides that he was sure would kill all the worms in his lawn. Fortunately, he had no pets or children as the warnings said the poison might prove harmful to them. He did give some momentary consideration to the birds, squirrels, and other wildlife in his area but decided his need to eliminate the worms was too great, and they would have to either survive or not on their own.

"Survival of the fittest," he said, "Darwin, baby, Darwin."

John purchased the necessary pesticide and generously spread it on his lawn as instructed, feeling confident that his driveway would be worm-free by the next heavy rainfall.

Periodically during the first several days after the initial application of the pesticide, John did find the occasional dead bird, chipmunk, or even stray cat on his lawn. As repulsed as he was by the discoveries, he somehow gathered the necessary strength to relegate the carcasses to his trash tub for weekly collection. He felt a bit like a ghoul lurking about in the dark, shoveling up the remains, stuffing them into a plastic garbage bag, then depositing them into his large trash receptacle.

Within a week or two, the animal deaths seemed to have stopped, and John assumed the pesticide had done its job. He supposed he'd find out soon. There were heavy summer rains predicted for the upcoming weekend. To everyone's surprise, not only was the rainstorm intense, but it was much more severe than anyone had anticipated and lasted for most of the weekend. Late that Sunday evening, John periodically went to his front window and looked at the driving rain as it pounded his neighborhood, sending deep streams of water cascading down the sides of his street while the storm drains struggled to keep flowing. John decided there was nothing for him to do but go to bed. He could check the status of his driveway early Monday morning when he left for work.

When he awoke, he noticed the rain had stopped, and it was an unusually still, quiet morning. He got ready for work then went out to survey the status of his driveway. To his pleasure, he saw the blacktop was completely clear and free of any worms. He could still smell a fishy scent in the air and had assumed the roads and everyone else's driveway had their share of the disgusting creatures. At least he had won his war against nature.

As he walked toward his car, John heard a strange wet sloshing sound. It reminded him of the sound a garden hose made when being pulled through wet leaves and grass. Then the fishy scent became even more intense. He turned and looked out into the early morning darkness at the street beyond. In the glow of the nearby streetlight, he saw something happening, which he knew was impossible.

Detritus from the storm covered the street. Branches, leaves, trash, undefinable refuse were everywhere. And worms, lots and lots of worms, all alive and squirming among the debris. Suddenly an icy fear stabbed its knives into John's belly. The mass of rubble in the street was somehow impossibly coming together, layer upon layer building higher and higher, all the while appearing to form something resembling a semi-humanoid shape.

"Golem" was the word that popped into John's mind. John had read about the mythical creatures of folklore which created themselves from dirt or mud. That was what he was seeing brought to life at the end of his driveway. The thing had grown to well over twelve feet tall, and even in the limited light, John could see the beast was being held into its form by thousands of squirming earthworms.

The hell-spawned beast turned its head in John's direction as it raised its arms high in the air. It opened its mouth and let loose with an ear-splitting, foul-smelling roar that shook John to the very core of his being. For a moment, he stood in shocked paralysis until the creature lifted its leg and dropped it to the wet street with a great pounding thump, which vibrated through John's body. It was then he knew why this Golem was there. It had come for him. The very creatures John had tried to eliminate now formed the beast.

Realizing the extent of his plight, John jumped into his car, slammed the door shut, put the car in reverse, and flew down the driveway determined to smash the monster back into the debris from which it arose. His vehicle slammed into the legs of the creature sending a shock wave through John's body. Then it stalled. He tried to restart it, but it wouldn't turn over. Looking in his rearview mirror, John saw as he had predicted the Golem had fallen to pieces. However, he hadn't anticipated what would happen next. The fragments of rubbish fell to the surface of his car and clung to it, rapidly forming a creeping shell around the vehicle.

The windows had become a thick opaque mass of remnants from the creature. Looking at the windshield, John saw bits of fur, feathers, and in some cases, complete carcasses of dead animals floating among the army of thousands of wriggling, squirming worms. Then the smell hit him like a slap in the face. It was the stench of dead animals, wet rotting leaves, and the fishy reek of worms.

He heard the sound of metal creaking as the cocoon began to tighten itself around the car. Then the first crack appeared in his windshield, followed by another, then another. Soon the car was filling with squirming, debris and John found himself up to his neck in the vile compost. He tried fruitlessly to get his door open. John desperately held his lips tightly together as the crawling mass slid all over his face. But when the worms began to climb into his nostrils, John found he had no choice but to breathe through his mouth. The nightmares of his suddenly became a reality as creatures squirmed over his lips and slithered down his throat. However, there would be no awakening from this horror.

BAIT AND SWITCH

"Bait the hook well. The fish will bite."
—William Shakespeare

"Do not bite at the bait of pleasure, till you know
there is no hook beneath it."
—Thomas Jefferson

"Look up ahead. There's bait active around that bend. We're bound to catch something good up there," the young girl said to her friend.

They were in the process of playing the latest and hottest augmented reality game known as Monster Mayhem. The game was just one of a dozen such games attracting a worldwide audience of gamers and making its developers millions of dollars. The competition required its players to go out into parks and other places to "capture" various digital monsters that appeared randomly. The couple was presently playing in a local museum park, and the sun was sinking low in the western sky.

There, of course, were all sorts of rules and a variety of weapons available to help capture the monsters. One such tool called "setting bait" allowed the player to place bait around one of the digital markers to attract monsters to that particular location.

"Yeah, but look around, Jill. It's getting dark, and there are no lights out this far."

"Seriously, Seth? Are you trying to tell me you're afraid of the dark?"

Seth found himself in a quandary. He liked Jill a lot. He hoped she might soon stop thinking of him as just a friend and maybe allow their relationship to take a more romantic turn. Perhaps this was just another teenage fantasy, but he was attracted to Jill. However, if he showed signs of being anything less than manly or protective, that opportunity might never come.

"Of course, I'm not! I'm not afraid of anything. It's just getting harder to see the path with just the minimal light from our phones. We left the blacktop a while back, and this path is nothing but dirt and gravel. I'm concerned you might trip, fall and hurt yourself."

"I'll be fine, Seth. Don't worry about me. Look, this is a city park, and there are dozens of people around here playing the game just like we are."

"I know, but they're far behind us now in the main part of the park where the light is. Nobody's way out here."

"Somebody is. Look at that bait on the screen Seth. That means someone had to set it up and he's likely out there right now getting tons of great monsters while we're standing here in the dark arguing. The clock is ticking, Seth. Baits are only good for like a half-hour, and we have no idea how long this one has been running."

Seth looked at his cell phone, "Oh great!"

"What?"

"Look at the name of the guy who set up the bait."

Jill looked at her phone and said, "It says 'Player Slayer.' So what?"

"Doesn't that nickname bother you? I mean, if this was a horror movie, we'd be screaming at the screen for the characters to turn tail and run. That name doesn't concern you even a little bit?"

"No, of course not. We all have goofy nicknames. Yours is 'Ultra Balls 2.' Tell me that isn't just a little bit vain."

"You know it isn't. I just took the name from the Ultra Balls we use in the game. That's all."

"Sure, you did. Now stop being so weird, Seth. Now let's go over there and see what we can catch."

"Fine, fine. But as soon as we get our share of monsters, we're heading back to civilization. Deal?"

"Sure, it's a deal. Now let's hurry."

The pair made their way along the path toward the area where the program's GPS screen showed the location of the bait. As they followed a curve in the walk, they came upon an open space with a wooden bench. There was no one in sight.

"This is the spot. Let's see what shows up," Jill suggested.

"Nobody's here, Jill. I wonder why 'Player Slayer' set the bait and then didn't stick around?"

"Geese, Seth. Stop worrying about dumb stuff. He could have set them up and gotten bored waiting for monsters to show up and just left. You know, some people have no patience, and sometimes it seems to take forever for monsters to be attracted to the bait. Look at your sightings bar, and you can see there are a couple of them nearby."

Seth looked down at his phone and said sarcastically. "Oh wow. Big fat deal! A Megadon, a Sykill and a Wolyhump. Boring! No wonder the guy abandoned this location. You can get those things all over the place and without wasting a single bait chip."

"Whatever, Seth. We're here, so let's give it a few minutes and see what else shows up?"

"Alright. But as soon as the bait runs down, we head back. Ok."

"Ok fine. Just stop bugging me about it. You're starting to work on my nerves."

Seth didn't reply. He knew Jill well enough to understand she was about to lose her temper, and she did have quite a spirited one indeed. Seth was starting to wonder if maybe his idea about making Jill his girlfriend was a bad idea after all. He had known her since they were toddlers. They had been together in every grade in school. That closeness combined with his raging hormones and Jill's blossoming figure and good looks had been the reason for his thoughts to turn to romance in the first place. But maybe he needed to rethink this course of action. She could be a real pain in the butt sometimes.

"Come on, Jill. This is a waste of time. Let's go."

"Ok, but just give it a minute. Something's bound to show up. I mean, come on. That's the whole purpose of setting bait in the first place."

"That's only partially true," A voice suddenly said from out of the darkness.

Instinctively, Jill reached over and grabbed Seth's hand. He felt warmth spread throughout his body at the excitement of her touch. Yet the fear, which was simultaneously shooting through him, overshadowed his momentary pleasure. He lifted his phone in the direction of the voice for light but couldn't see anyone there.

The voice continued, "Yes. You can set the bait to attract monsters for you to hunt in your game. But bait can also serve other purposes."

A pair of legs clothed in dark black jeans and dark boots stepped into the light of Seth's phone. Seth raised the light slowly along the stranger's body and saw the man wore a black tee-shirt and a long black leather coat. He had on a dark black wide-brimmed hat, which shielded his downturned face. But Seth could see the man had a heavy black beard.

"You know, a lot of people think this whole Monster Mayhem game is just a fad and is stupid and ridiculous. In some ways, they may be right. However, I've discovered these sorts of games can serve many good purposes. They get people, especially kids, off the sofa. You can't be a couch potato and play these games. You have to get up and get out of the house. I'm sure you're aware we have become such a sedentary society. The players get to walk around and get good exercise while enjoying an interesting game. They also get to meet and interact with other players in real life, face-to-face rather than sitting at home in front of some video screen talking to unseen players over a headset. I think those are all good things. Wouldn't you agree?"

Neither of them responded. Jill squeezed Seth's hand even tighter. The man raised his head, and Seth heard Jill gasp next to him. Scars rippled the stranger's face appearing as if he had survived a bad burn and his eyes seemed to glow with an intensity that suggested a madness living somewhere deep within him. The man opened his mouth in a deranged smile, revealing a maw filled with brown and rotting teeth. He barely looked human at all. He was more like one of the monsters from the game.

"But you see, bait can also serve another purpose. You can use bait to attract game players like the both of you. And as my game name Player-Slayer suggests, I enjoy hunting you much more than the fictional game characters."

The last thing Jill and Seth saw in their young lives was the long, sharp sword blade glimmering in the light from their cell phones as the weapon of death came slashing down toward them.

THE HORTON MOUNTAIN GHOST

The Ford Econoline van carrying the Daley family traveled over Horton Mountain on that Friday night in late October 1969. The Daley children were riveted, sitting silently as their father George Daley recounted the chilling details behind a local ghost legend using his most sinister voice.

"The young woman's burned body was found in the woods by two hikers, way back in 1925, not very far from where we are right now. They never identified the woman or her killers."

"Honestly, George, do you think that's an appropriate story to be telling the children?" Laura Daley chastised her husband.

"Of course, it is. It's honest-to-goodness local history."

Then once again giving his voice a mysterious tone, he delivered the final blow, "And now it's said her ghost wanders the top of this mountain on nights, much like this one, looking for her killers. Sometimes she causes cars passing by to lose power, and she walks up to their widows and looks inside."

Without warning, he pulled the van over to the side of the road, shut off the engine, and said, "Hey, what's wrong with the van?"

The children began to stir uncomfortably.

Laura admonished, "That's not very funny, George."

"Something's wrong with the van," George explained, then he shouted, "Oh my God! Look out there! What's that?"

Two yellow eyes glowed up ahead in the luminescence of the van's headlights.

"It's her. There she is, kids! The Horton Mountain Ghost. And now she's coming for you!"

The four Daley kids dove to the floor of the van amid a cacophony of screams. The two brothers, Will and Jack, ages four and six respectively, were flat on the floor with their hands clapped firmly over their heads, trembling in fear with their eyes squeezed tightly shut. Their next older sister Joanie, age nine, was screaming and crying uncontrollably. The oldest daughter, Linda, who was twelve, was doing her best to pretend she wasn't frightened and was only playing along. However, in the back of her mind, she felt uncertain and even a bit worried.

"Oh, George, now you've done it! You've scared the children half to death!" Laura scolded, "Kids, don't be upset; it's only a deer. Take a look, and you'll see. For Heaven's sake, George!"

Slowly, one by one, the children rose from the limited security of the van's floor to look out the window. Joanie was the last to look as her hysterical outbursts always took the longest to calm down. A large buck stepped out of darkness and proceeded to cross the highway. George laughed hysterically, pounding on the steering wheel at the joke he had played on his kids.

"Daddy, that wasn't funny!" Joanie shouted between sobs. "You scared us bad."

Trying to regain his composure, George said, "I'm so sorry, Sweetie. I couldn't resist. It was just such perfect timing."

Laura said, "Sometimes you can be very nasty, George Daley. You should be ashamed of yourself, scaring your children like that."

"I wasn't scared. I don't believe in ghosts," Linda announced proudly.

Still trembling, Joanie argued, "You were too scared, Linda. You were right down there on the floor with us."

"I was just playing along so you kids wouldn't be any more scared than you already we're."

Jack said, "That was mean, Daddy, but kinda cool too." He was smiling enthusiastically.

Little Will said nothing. He just sat staring out the window. He was neither smiling nor laughing as the buck crossed the roadway and disappeared back into the woods on the opposite side.

"Well, we best be on our way," George said after a moment as he started the van and pulled back out onto the highway.

Three of the children were now nervously chuckling about what had just happened, but not little Will. He was staring in shocked silence out the side window at two glowing eyes peering in from a burned and scarred face.

PEOPLE ARE STRANGE

People are strange when you're a stranger;
faces look ugly when you're alone.
—JIM MORRISON

As he stepped through the brass doors into the lobby of the Greenwood Suites Hotel, he heard the tinny ringing of the bell stationed above the door. He instantly sensed something was very wrong. The hall, although spacious, was not at all what he expected. Walden Jacobs had been a business traveler throughout his professional life, and usually, hotels were bustling. Since this was the only decent hotel in this small Mississippi town, he would have expected to see many people milling about.

However, the hotel was silent and empty save for the rail-thin female desk attendant standing behind the front counter; she was dressed in a worn sundress and was staring oddly at him. Walden thought perhaps a simple welcoming greeting might be in order. However, the young woman stood silently gawking at him with her mouth hanging open in a hang-dog fashion that made her appear to be mentally deficient, which Walden suspected might be the case.

Walden felt a cold sweat of discomfort trickling down the center of his back. He cautiously approached the registration counter. Walden hesitated, waiting for her to do something. When she didn't, he elected to speak up, "I'm here to check in. Reservation is in the name Jacobs, Walden Jacobs."

The woman said nothing then picked up an envelope with a hotel brochure and a room key. On the outside of the envelope, Walden saw the name "W. Jacobs" and the room number "413."

"Is there an elevator nearby? He asked. He wondered why she put him all the way up on the fourth floor in a hotel that was almost empty.

The woman continued to stare strangely at him for a time. Then she half-heartedly looked in the direction of a hallway off to the right. Before Walden could thank her, he discovered the clerk had turned and walked away into a back office.

Walden thought, "What a strange woman. I wonder what her problem is."

He had always heard positive things about southern hospitality, but this woman had been anything but hospitable.

After putting his luggage into his unremarkable room, Walden decided to go out and find a place to get dinner. Generally, in a fine hotel, he would ask the concierge for a recommendation. Or, in the case of a lesser quality hotel, Walden would inquire at the front desk. But he knew neither was an option here.

Instead, Walden picked up a local hotel courtesy magazine from the room's desk and flipped through the pages looking for someplace special. He found a place called Bob's BBQ, which boasted of fine down-home barbecue.

Walden left his room and took the elevator down to the first floor. He walked past the check-in desk and noticed the same woman standing and staring at him. Walden didn't bother to comment but headed out to his car. He could feel her eyes boring a hole in him the entire time. In his mind, he heard a female voice saying, "You're a stranger. You're not from around here." He glanced back at the woman but saw once again she had left her post.

On his way to Bob's BBQ, Walden decided to stop for gas at the only combination gas station and mini-mart in town. It wasn't part of any national chain but was a mom-and-pop store called Gertie's. It was the sort of place that Walden suspected divided refrigerator space between cold foods and fish bate.

The gas pumps did not allow remote payment by credit card, so Walden had to go inside to prepay. He made a note of the number on the pump. As he walked in the door, an overhead bell tinkled, signaling his arrival. As with the hotel, it caught him off guard. It sounded just like the bell at the hotel.

To his right, he saw a line of well-worn booths for in-store dining, all occupied by a half dozen of what Walden was certain were locals, all of them men in a variety of shabby work clothing. Some of the men wore tattered truckers' hats. They all looked up at the sound of the bell. Looking from man to man Walden realized they all had the same dull eyes and drooping lower jaw as the girl at the hotel.

As Walden walked up to the service counter, he felt a dozen eyes staring at him. No one spoke, but, in his mind, he could hear deep male voices saying, "You're a stranger. You're not from around here. We don't like strangers."

Ignoring his growing feeling of dread, Waldon stared across the service counter into the hooded eyes of a haggard-looking woman in her forties or fifties. She wore a frayed, faded green and yellow sundress adorned with several unidentifiable stains. The woman bore a striking resemblance to the girl at the hotel desk. She could have passed for her mother or older sister. Her face had the same dull slack-jawed expression. Now that he thought about it, those guys seated at the booths all looked similar as well.

"Inbreeding gone wild," he thought. Then he recalled a line from some bad southern joke he had once heard, "I'd like you to meet my Uncle Daddy." He held back a chuckle when thinking of the snarky comment. He was not among friends here; that was plain to see.

"I'd like twenty dollars' worth of gas on pump three," he said, handing the woman his credit card.

She stood staring at him for a moment as if not comprehending what he had said. Walden felt like she was taking each word of his sentence and running it through some sort of translator. After a time, she slowly took his credit card and ran it through her card reader. Without saying a word, the woman handed the card back along with a slip for him to sign. Walden did so without looking up because he sensed she was still gawking at him with those hooded, mentally deficient eyes.

As he signed the bill, he heard a female voice inside his head say, "You're a stranger. You're not from around here. We don't like strangers. We kill strangers."

Walden's heart skipped a beat as he said, "Excuse me. Did you just say something?"

The woman seemed not to hear him as she turned and began transferring cigarettes from a box on the dirty vinyl floor to their appropriate locations on a metal cigarette rack. Walden knew without turning around, the men behind him were still staring at him. He opted to turn and leave the store, avoiding eye contact with these "local mutants" as he passed. Walden returned to the pumps and began filling his tank. It wasn't cold that evening, but he felt chilled, nonetheless. He ventured a glance at the store window, and as he dreaded, all of the men seated at the booths were watching him.

With great relief, Walden got into his car and pulled away quickly. He took the opportunity to give a single-finger salute to the mini-mart as he did. Looking in his rearview mirror, Walden saw the clerk in her frumpy sundress standing outside the store with a cigarette burning between her fingers, still staring intently at him. The chill worsened, and he shivered as he recalled the words he had just heard in his mind. Was that voice the woman's voice, or had he imagined the whole thing?

Why would these people, total strangers, want to kill him? He obviously must be letting the weirdness of the town and its people get the best of him. They were just simple folk, nothing more. Maybe he'd feel better after a few drinks and some good old-fashioned down-home cooking. He pulled his rental into the parking lot in front of Bob's BBQ and made up his mind to put all of his uneasiness behind him, relax and enjoy dinner.

Bob's was an old wood-framed structure that had seen better days. The sign mounted over the front porch was faded and barely legible. It had a neon sign hanging in the front window reading "OP N," the "E" conspicuously burned out. The place was painted a dull gray or had been a long time ago. Now, however, the paint was faded, chipped, and peeling. Walden opened one of the two wooden front doors and heard a familiar sound that startled him. It was the ringing of an overhead bell. Its sound wasn't just similar to those at the hotel and mini-mart but identical.

He walked into the restaurant and passed a sign reading "Please Seat Yourself," making his way to one of the empty tables. Couples occupied many of the tables. Their appearance not only screamed "locals," but Walden was shocked to notice once again how much they all looked like everyone else he had seen in this strange town.

Walden thought, "Is everyone in this town related or what?"

He sat down and grabbed one of the menus stacked behind the metal napkin dispenser. He pretended to study it intently when in reality, he was trying to decide whether to get up and casually stroll out of the restaurant or run away like a crazy man. The place was giving him the creeps, big time. Before he had an opportunity to make his getaway, he felt someone standing nearby and glanced to his left to see his waitress standing by his table.

Usually, this was where the woman would say something like, "I'm Daisy Mae, and I'll be your server." However, this woman said nothing. She just stood silently. He turned his head fully to better look at the woman, and a gasp caught in his throat. If he didn't know better, he would have thought the woman from the mini-mart had somehow run the three miles to Bob's BBQ and quickly slipped into a waitress uniform; the kind Walden hadn't seen except in old movies from the 1950s and '60s. She looked identical to the woman from Gertie's.

Walden felt like he was in the middle of a nightmare and didn't know what to do next. He supposed he should place his order. That's what someone would do in a sane world. But everything was so surreal and bizarre that he was unable to think straight, let alone speak.

That was when he heard a chorus of voices in his head saying, "You're a stranger. You're not from around here. We don't like strangers. We kill strangers. We eat strangers."

Then as if instructed by some unspoken command, everyone in the restaurant rose simultaneously and surrounded Walden's table. Still trying to comprehend what was happening, Walden looked up into their gaunt faces with their dull hooded eyes and mouths hanging open. But now, in those eyes, he saw something else; hunger. And those mouths were open wide, displaying rotting tombstone teeth. And as they reached their thin arms and long bony fingers toward him, he knew what the main course was for the evening.

JACOB'S TREE

The old tree stood alone on an island of dirt in the middle of the corn-field, the only tree remaining of the original crop of more than a dozen. The others had all died out over the years. With its gnarled, twisted trunk and dried-out branches, this tree looked as though it would soon be joining its brothers in death. Scores of crows flew through the fields but seemed to do their best to avoid the tree. Perhaps this was because the tree resembled a giant scarecrow, or perhaps for other reasons only they knew.

Jessica had never understood why these strange islands of trees and underbrush appeared scattered throughout various farm fields. She always thought a more open uninterrupted area would make the farmer's job a lot easier. That was until Jacob had explained it to her.

He had told her, "Sometimes the trees act as wind barriers. If you plant the right vegetation among the trees, it can lure insects away from the crops. And sometimes, especially in the old days, these areas even served as family burial grounds."

Jacob had been the fourth-generation son of a farming family. He also considered himself Jessica's fiancé, although she would be almost certain to disagree. Their relationship was rocky at times and complicated at others. They had been friends since junior high school. Even back then, in the eighth grade, Jacob announced he would marry Jessica someday. She never thought he was serious, even though he continued to insist they would marry all through high school.

Jessica liked Jacob a lot, but only as a friend. It wasn't like they had ever actually dated or, for that matter, had even kissed. In her mind, they were just good friends. Jessica had big plans for her future. She was going to go away to college. After that, Jessica hoped to land a high-paying job somewhere far away and would never return. She knew she could never settle down and be content to be a farmer's wife, pumping out a brood of farm kids. She tried to explain this to Jacob, time and time again, but he wouldn't listen.

"It's our destiny to be together, Jessica," he would insist. "You can say what you want and believe whatever you choose, but I know it's you and me forever."

No matter how much Jacob frustrated her with his endless talk of love and marriage, Jessica never dared to say the words Jacob needed to hear. She honestly didn't want to hurt him, but somehow, she had to find a way to get him to understand. Jessica did her best to avoid him during the final months of high school. She had thought perhaps this cold shoulder treatment would be a subtle way of not only distancing herself from Jacob but maybe making him lose interest in her as well. She thought her plan was working until a week or so after high school graduation.

She came out of a clothing store at the local shopping center when Jacob pulled over to the curb in his pickup truck and asked her to get in.

"Sorry Jacob, I can't now. I have things to do," she told him.

Jacob gave her that lost puppy look She had once found cute but now just found annoying, "Come on, Jessica. It's stupid to be avoiding me this way, especially with us getting married and all."

"For the last time, Jacob, we're not getting married," she said, trying to remain calm but feeling her temper growing.

"But of course, we are. We've been talking about this for years."

"No, WE haven't, Jacob, you have. Not us, just you. I'm not marrying you or anyone else. I'm leaving for college out of state in two months and never coming back here!"

"But, Jess, you and I have to start making babies, lots of them. And we can't do that without getting married."

"You're such a dope, Jacob. You don't have to be married to have babies or to have sex."

"Maybe not everybody, but I do, Jess. That's how we do things around here. You know that. That's why we've been saving ourselves for marriage all these years."

Jessica went suddenly silent and had trouble meeting Jacob's stern gaze. Jacob said, "Jess? You, you have been saving yourself, haven't you?"

She knew her answer would break Jacob's heart, but she had no choice. He wouldn't leave her alone. She took a deep breath and murmured, "No, Jacob, I haven't saved myself for marriage or you. There have already been many boys. I'm sorry, Jacob, but that's just the way it is."

Jacob looked as if Jessica had reached inside his chest and pulled out his still-beating heart, crushing it between her fingers. He never said another word to her; he just turned his head away and drove off. She never spoke to him again. Two weeks later, Jacob died while working on the farm in an accident involving a piece of heavy equipment.

His parents had his body cremated and his ashes scattered beneath the old, twisted tree on the island in the cornfield. Jessica attended his memorial service held at the tree's base. Jacob's parents spread his ashes there among the dirt. After that day, she always thought of the hideous tree as Jacob's tree.

Jessica spent the rest of the summer getting ready for college. Occasionally she had made a few trips past the cornfield where Jacob's tree stood but never left her car or ventured out to the island. She would often imagine him saying to her, "It's our destiny to be together forever." But she always managed to put the thoughts out of her mind.

Except for those creeping thoughts of Jacob, that summer was an exciting time for her as it marked the start of her adult life. She was going away to college. She was going to make her life something special. Nevertheless, every so often, she would still hear Jacob's voice in the back of her mind saying, "It's our destiny to be together forever."

The day before she was to leave for college Jessica realized she needed to find closure. She had to find a way to put Jacob and her past to rest before she could begin her new life.

She drove out to Jacob's family farm and parked along the dirt road leading back to his parents' farmhouse. She crawled over the split-rail fence and walked out to the island and Jacob's tree.

She stood before the gnarled and twisted thing and said, "Jacob. I'm so, so sorry. I tried to explain to you for years that we could only be friends. I should have been more honest with you, but I didn't want to hurt you or risk our friendship. But in the end, I lost you, and for that, I will be sorry for the rest of my life."

"It's our destiny to be together forever, Jessica."

Jessica's breath caught in her throat as she heard Jacob's voice again, more clearly than in the past. She was sure she not only heard the voice in her mind but in her ears as well. Yet, she knew such a thing was impossible. That was when she heard a scraping sound like some creeping creature slithering along the ground. She looked down and saw several long vines rising from the ground at the base of the tree and working their way toward her ankles. She stood stunned for a moment then began to slowly back up.

As she did, she felt something press hard against her back and looked up to see the tree leaning down toward her with its long branches extended like twisted arms. She saw a face forming on the surface of the tree's weathered bark. It was Jacob's face. She felt her chest tighten and saw some of the smaller branches had grabbed her around the waist and chest. They were like solid hands, their grip vice-like, driving the air from her lungs.

Within seconds she was lifted high into the air and brought toward the tree trunk, where she was held tightly by branches and vines. Soon the creeping foliage had encircled her, tearing off her clothes and leaving her naked and bruised in its grip. As she hung in the air, she felt the vines crawling up her legs and invading her most private of areas. She burned with unbearable pain. She wanted to scream out, but more of the invasive things had found their way into her mouth and were crawling down her throat, choking off her air supply.

As nightfall engulfed the remainder of the day, Jacob's tree swallowed Jessica, bringing her back to him. Her last thoughts were that Jacob was right. She would now be his forever.

MORE THAN A FEELING

He told no one of his irrational fear; at least, he preferred to believe the fear was irrational. But that knowledge did little to make the anxiety cease when it chose to make its presence known. At those times, it seemed as natural as anything he had ever experienced in his life. Thank goodness, it only happened maybe once or twice a year, and always around the same time in late October, on or near Halloween.

He never told anyone about it because he wasn't sure how to explain the sensation, especially since he didn't understand it. After almost sixty years of dealing with it, he thought of it as a sort of waiting. He was waiting for something, but what exactly he didn't know; he just intuitively understood it was something terrible. He knew what signs to watch out for, and as such, he could sense its approach. It didn't seem to matter where he was at the time or even in which part of the country he happened to be. He had moved several times to different parts of the United States during his lifetime, but nothing he did could stop the feeling from returning; the waiting. For a time, during his mid-forties, he had considered speaking with a psychiatrist to get a professional's take on his situation but eventually thought better of it and didn't bother.

He tried to come up with reasons on his own for the feeling, wondering if perhaps as a child, he had been frightened on Halloween night, and although likely a suppressed memory, the unsettling feeling still manifested at that time of year. Yet, he couldn't recall any such childhood trauma no matter how hard he tried. On the other hand, maybe it was simply the nature of the holiday itself with all the scary costumes and general thoughts of evil demons roaming about in the darkness.

Of course, he didn't believe in ghosts, ghouls, monsters, or goblins, and such, but still, maybe they caused some involuntary sensations of unrest and waiting to overtake him. It might even be the stillness of autumn, the leaves dying, withering, and falling from the trees, leaving them skeletal remnants of what they once had been. Maybe even the smells of fall and the decomposing foliage signaling the cold bleakness of the coming winter.

However, he didn't believe any of that was the case. The waiting was something else, something much more primal, something that made the hairs on the back of his neck tingle. It was a feeling, which made his stomach lurch and his legs tremble. It was much more than just a feeling or a sensation. Nothing so trivial could bring on such utter terror or have such a debilitating effect.

He had learned to watch for the signs, anticipate its arrival, and deal with the results. Now all these years later, he felt he might be close to the point where he was beginning to feel its crippling effects dwindling. Over the past decade or so, whenever the sensation arrived, his heart pounded less. Likewise did the tingling feeling, which always seemed to snake down his spine like a thousand insects scurrying down his back.

During the past few years, the cold sweats had practically ceased entirely. Perhaps the waiting feeling was gone. That would soon become apparent as it was the morning of October 31, and so far, he hadn't had even the slightest hint that the feeling might be coming his way. He had been up for work at 4:30 am, as usual, dressed for work and out the door by 5:25. He did what he did every morning before leaving and went to the mailbox to retrieve the morning newspaper.

He reached into the newspaper tube only to discover it was empty. "Hum?" He thought, "The paper must be late today."

Then before he had a chance to complete that thought, the feeling hit him without warning like a club to the side of his skull. The anticipation seemed more crippling than anything he had ever previously experienced. It was all-encompassing and overwhelming.

He stood with his hand still in the empty newspaper tube, practically paralyzed with fear. A doctor had been treating him for high blood pressure for several years, then for a brief moment; he wondered just how high it had gotten within the last few seconds. He could feel his heart practically jumping in his chest, and the inside of his head seemed to thump painfully with every beat of his pounding heart.

He managed to draw his hand slowly from the tube and turn to his left to look down the darkened suburban street, poorly illuminated only by a few strategically placed pole lights. Although very decorative and quite attractive, they failed to provide sufficient lighting. A thick, fast-moving fog had suddenly formed far down the street and appeared to be rolling toward him at an incredible speed.

Before he realized it, the fog had utterly engulfed him. It was so thick he could no longer see the mailbox, which he knew to be right in front of him. He had no idea what was happening but knew the waiting feeling was responsible. That moment he understood was the moment he had both waited for and dreaded all of his life. What was happening to him was not just the feeling but something much, much more. It was as if all those years, the waiting had been some sort of precognitive warning of what was to come someday. And he knew for sure something was coming, and whatever it was would be arriving at any second. Then he heard a scraping sound coming from somewhere out in the fog, a low-to-the-ground skeletal scratching.

Slowly the fog began to dissipate directly in front of him, and he saw something coming along the ground toward him. At first, he thought it might be an animal of some sort, like a stray dog, because he believed he could see what resembled a fur-covered back crouching low to the ground. But as he looked closer, he could see flesh-colored tentacles moving in a coordinated fashion underneath the body of whatever it was that he was seeing. He sensed these limbs must be the propulsion system the creature used to move. He knew the logical thing to do was to turn and try to flee. However, he instinctively understood that there would be nowhere for him to hide. He had anticipated this for fifty-nine years. Whatever it was that was supposed to happen, it would be happening very soon.

The slow-moving shadowy figure got closer. There was a moist, sweat-like sheen across the skin's surface, glimmering in the minimal light available on the street. Although the manner of the beast was indistinguishable, he knew it was responsible for the feeling, and it was there for him. This sensation was no longer just a waiting feeling; it was reality.

Without warning, the creature somehow unbelievably raised on a pair of muscular human-like hind legs, which he hadn't noticed earlier. Its underbelly was pink and slimy, consisting of what seemed like dozens of long tentacles. But there was something else as well, something horrifying located right in its center. It was some sort of unbelievable mouth about two feet in diameter and encircled with what appeared to be hundreds if not thousands of long, inward-curving fangs. At the center of the circular maw, a thick pink tongue protruded out into the air as if sensing him standing close by. Above the thing's mouth contained a series of perhaps twenty fleshy extensions with eyeballs at their ends, similar to those of a snail or slug.

Now mesmerized, he felt both mentally and physically numb, which, as it turned out, was probably for the best. Because within the next second, at unimaginable speed, the tentacles shot outward, grabbing him, pulling him hard toward the giant slurping mouth.

During the last terrifying moments of his life, all of the sensitivity had left his body. This lack of feeling became a blessing because those hundreds of razor-sharp fangs had begun chewing through his flesh as the creature pulled him further into the gaping hole of a mouth. The last thoughts he had before his life ended surprised him. He was wondering why he had worried for fifty-nine years about the waiting. Now that this day had finally come, it strangely wasn't as bad as he had thought it would be after all. Death was just seconds away, and after a lifetime of waiting, fearing the unknown, the time had finally come, the waiting was over at last, and it was something of a relief.

REVOLTING CANDY COMPANY

The red "recording" light glowed brightly in the dimness of the radio studio as the engineer signaled the final three-second silent count down by lowering each of his fingers. A sign illuminated proclaiming "On Air" as the host began to speak.

"Good evening, ladies and gentlemen, and welcome to *Amazing People,*" the show that goes above and beyond to bring you a look into the lives of today's movers, shakers, and newsmakers. My name is Brandon Fisker, and I'm the creator and not so humble host of this incredible program.

"Tonight, we have an extraordinary guest joining me live on the air. He is someone I've wanted to have in my studio for many years. Sitting across the desk from me this evening is none other than the legendary and always controversial Mr. Homer T. McCabe, president, CEO, and creative genius behind the Revolting Candy Company.

"This is indeed a rare and special opportunity as the normally somewhat reclusive multimillionaire has agreed to sit down and speak to us. Isn't that right, Mr. McCabe?"

"Um . . . yes, yes it is. But please call me Homer."

"Very well, Homer. First, let me thank you for taking the time out of your busy schedule to talk with me. The Revolting Candy Company has become one of the most successful candy companies in American history. It's also both loved and despised by equal numbers of people.

Well, as they say, time is money. So, let's get right to it. I guess the best way to get this interview off the ground is to get some of the preliminary info and background history out of the way. You started the Revolting Candy Company in 1983 in your parents' basement, is that correct?"

"Yes, that is correct indeed. I had this idea to make incredibly tasting candies that people would love but give them names and appearances that under other circumstances, would be considered revolting and might even turn their stomachs."

"That sounds like it was a precarious endeavor to me, Homer."

"It was. My parents thought I was out of my mind when I dropped out of college and borrowed $500 from the bank using my beat-up 1976 Ford sedan as collateral. My folks were sure I'd lose the car in a month and end up living in their basement for the rest of my life."

"How do they feel about things now?" Brandon asked.

"I think they feel pretty convinced I should be ok for a while. At least that's what the folks told me last time I visited them at their home in Key West."

"I've heard that home is a sprawling estate worth over five million dollars. You bought them that home, didn't you?"

Homer said, "It's the least I could do for them. After all, they're my parents. Plus, they supported me and my crazy ideas when I was getting the company off the ground."

"Amazing. Now let's talk a bit about the products your company produces. What was your first offering? What was the first product you came up with?"

"Well, Brandon, I had several ideas for products simultaneously but knew I only had sufficient capital to produce one."

Brandon asked, "Would that be the famous Litter Box Crunchies?"

"Yes, it certainly would be. I had already developed my formula for my special brand of chocolate. However, I decided rather than market it in any of the traditional shapes. I got a great idea that to form this candy into shapes resembling cat turds. Yeah, I know how that sounds. Then I took some crushed Rice Crispies and some granulated sugar and coated the chocolate with it making it look like something that had just rolled out of the litter box. Hence the name Litterbox Crunchies."

Brandon said, "And that became one of your biggest sellers to date, isn't that correct?"

"Yes, it is. We even pack the candy m in litter box-shaped packaging. Unfortunately, we then tried to follow up on that success of the cat turds with a 'human' version of the crunchies," Homer said, making air quotes around 'human,' which of course no one but Brandon could see. "We put peanuts inside the chocolate to sort of expanding on the joke, but they weren't very well received. We may have been trying to push the envelope a bit too far back then. I suppose it's good I didn't go with my original plan to put candy corn inside."

"Um, yes, that probably wouldn't have been very popular. I assume the product you're referring to was what you had called Rectum Rippers?" Brandon said, realizing what a bizarre discussion they were having. However, he had waited so many years for this chance. He needed to keep his guest happy, at least for a while.

"Yes. Unfortunately, Rippers were a bit ahead of their time. But the world has changed significantly over the last decade, and I predict Rectum Rippers will be making a comeback very soon."

"Remember folks," Brandon said, addressing his radio audience. You heard it here first on Amazing People. Rectum Rippers will be coming out soon. Oh, I suppose I should have worded that differently. Anyway, Homer, after the failure of the initial release of Rectum Rippers, your company nearly went bankrupt, is that correct?"

"Well, yes, Brandon, that, unfortunately, is very true. We went through a rough patch there for a while. But luckily, the Litter Box Crunchies were still selling like crazy, and that revenue is what saved the company."

"What happened next? What direction did you take the company after that?"

"Well, I had this idea for gummy candies shaped like boogers. I figured we could make them all various shades of green, regardless of their flavor. Every candy flavor would be a surprise. I decided to call them Surprise Sugar Boogers."

"As I recall, they proved to be a great hit as well," Brandon said, "Whose idea was it to package them in a soft plastic nose dispenser?"

"That was my idea too, Brandon. I figured it would be cool for the kids to squeeze the nose and have the candies dribble out the nostrils."

"Genius, pure genius! It's like everything you touch turns into money."

"Well, not everything Brandon. Besides the fiasco over the Rectum Rippers, we've had our share of other flops. For example, the Fruit Flavored Fetus line was a complete disaster."

"Oh yeah, I was eventually going to get around to mentioning those. You got a lot of bad press over that particular product line, as I recall."

"Yes, I suppose you could say that. The right-to-lifers burned me in effigy plenty of times during protests. I had truck-loads of hate mail over my fetuses and more than my share of death threats."

"Seriously? Actual death threats?"

"Oh yes. People, especially women, get a bit hostile when you make light of their ability to give birth, or so I learned the hard way. But at least something good came out of all that hassle in the end."

"And what was that?" Brandon asked.

"Well, during one of the protest demonstrations, a group of angry women had a dummy which was supposed to represent me. There was this one woman, a real man-hater if you know what I mean, who coated the dummy's crotch with some sort of accelerant and lit it on fire. My marketing manager watched from my office window and said something like, 'Wow, look at that! She's roasting your nuts, Homer.'"

Brandon asked, "You mean to tell me . . ."

"Yep, that was the inspiration for our line of Homer's Candy Coated Roasted Nuts. I came up with the idea of packaging them in the wrinkled flesh-colored nut sack as well."

"Again. Pure genius. So, what do you think Homer, are you ready to take some calls from our listeners?"

"Sure thing Brandon. I'm always ready, but I should warn you, you might not be ready. Sometimes these things get a bit out of control. There's a reason I'm reluctant to interact with the general public."

"I assume you mean because of the controversial nature of your company?"

"Yes, I suppose that's right. Although I never understood why people consider my company or my ideas controversial. I mean, it's not like we're hiding behind some cutesy mainstream company name like Sweetie Pie Sweets Company or something like that. I mean, if a company is called The Revolting Candy Company, what else should you expect?"

"I agree with you there, Homer, but there are different degrees of disgust, and people tend to determine their acceptance or rejection on an individual basis. For example, the idea of gummy boogers might seem funny to one person, yet another might become nauseated at the very mention of such an idea. But enough of this, let's talk to our first caller. We have Jason from Baltimore, Maryland. Go ahead, caller; you're on the air."

"Hey, Brandon. I'm a big fan of your show and a first-time caller."

"Thanks, Jason. Much appreciated. So, what's your question for Homer?"

"Um . . . ah . . . sorry, I'm a bit nervous. Um, Homer, who came up with the idea to take white chocolate, melt it around various candy bits, and to make it look like a pile of vomit?"

"You're referring to our Pukie Puddles. Yeah, that one was mine too."

Brandon said, "See what I'm saying, people, this man is a genius! No. You know what? Genius doesn't cut it. This man is a God among men. Wouldn't you agree, Jason?"

"Yes, most definitely. Homer's ideas are amazing."

"Thanks, Jason. I couldn't have said it better myself. We don't call this show *Amazing People* for nothing,"

"That certainly went much better than I thought it would," Homer said quietly to the host.

Brandon said, "Now let's go to our next caller. We have Mary from Kansas City, Missouri. Go ahead, Mary, ask your question."

"How the hell can you sleep at night, McCabe? You're the most disgusting degenerate ever. Litter Box Crunchies? Rectum Rippers?

Seriously? These names sound like something a fifteen-year-old might think up. For God's sake, grow up! Your ideas are revolting, and your candy tastes like crap!"

Homer looked slyly at Brandon, winked, and asked the caller, "So would you care to share with us exactly how you know what crap tastes like?"

Brandon realized he was about to see first-hand something he had suspected for some time. He knew you didn't get to that level of financial success Homer McCabe had reached unless you had a natural killer instinct. He might appear to be a reclusive genius on the surface, but when push came to shove, he went right for the jugular, as Brandon always suspected.

Homer caught the caller off guard. "Wa . . . what are you saying? I don't understand what you're asking me?"

"Well, you said my candy tastes like crap, and I was wondering how exactly you knew how crap tastes? I mean, it's not every day you get to meet someone who likes to sit down with a bowl of the stuff. Tell me, do you like to sample your own, or do you prefer to dine out?"

"Oh my God!" The woman exclaimed, "You truly are as despicable as your vile and revolting candies!"

"Well ma'am, my company is called the Revolting Candy Company after all. As I said before, what do you expect?"

"What do I expect? I expect . . . I expect you to go to Hell."

The woman slammed down her phone, causing a loud noise to echo through Brandon's and Homer's headsets.

"Well, that was more like what I expected," Homer said. "As you can see, people can be quite adamant about their feelings toward my company. Some people are rabid fans, and others are just rabid."

Brandon said, "Wow, that was something! I'd normally thank her for the call, but she was quite rude."

"Now you know why so tend to avoid these sorts of on-air call-in shows. Nothing good ever comes of them. Sure, you get the occasional fan and maybe the random compliment, but for the most part, we get angry turd-nibbling mutants like that last caller."

Brandon was once again caught off guard by the amount of ferocity Homer so quickly had unleashed upon the woman. Had he just called her a turd-nibbling mutant?

"I must say you, um, held your own quite well in that encounter. You've had your share of experience. Well, I suppose that's why the woman chose to disconnect the call. What say we try another?" Brandon suggested, "We have a caller waiting from Ashton, Pennsylvania. I don't believe I ever heard of that town."

Homer said, "Actually, Ashton is the town where I was born and where I went to school until my parents moved us to Pittsburgh just before my senior year."

"Wow. That must have been tough leaving all your friends behind. Then you had to move to the opposite side of the state so late in your education."

Homer hesitated for a moment as if recalling an unpleasant memory, then said, "It was rough for a while. After we moved, I was new and had no friends. I spent all of my time working on my ideas for the candy company. If it wasn't for the move, this company might never have happened."

"Wow, what a great bit of information for our listening audience! Go ahead, caller. We have Alecia from Ashton, PA, on the line. What's your question, Alecia?"

A low, humming sound came over the speaker, followed by intermittent bursts of static.

"Hello? Alecia? Are you still on the line Alecia? What's your question, Alecia?"

In the background, they could hear their voices coming through the phone saying things they said earlier.

Brandon shouted, "You have to turn down your radio, Alecia. There's a seven-second delay, and I believe it's confusing you."

After a few seconds, the line got quiet, and Brandon said in a much calmer voice, "There, that's much better. Now can you tell me what question you had for Homer T. McCabe?"

"Question?" A small, barely audible voice said through their head-phones, "For Homer?" The vocal tone had a strange, almost ethereal quality to it.

"Um yes, Alecia," Brandon said with apparently forced patience, "You called into this show, and usually when someone does that, they want to ask a question. So, what's yours?"

The phone was silent for a few seconds, and Brandon was about to say something to avoid an automatic dead air warning when the voice spoke again.

"My question for Homer is . . . why . . . why did you kill me, Homer?"

"Excuse me," Brandon asked, visibly shocked, "What did you just say?"

"I asked why Homie killed me. I always used to call him Homie back when we were kids. He liked that. Isn't that right, Homie?"

Homer sat up in his seat, shouting to Brandon, "This is the sort of call I was warning you about. An obvious crank call; some weirdo's idea of a joke. I think you should hang up on her immediately."

Homer stared sternly at the host. Why wasn't he disconnecting the call?

"Alecia? Can you tell me how old you are?" Brandon asked.

"I'm fifteen," She said.

"Can you tell me your last name?"

"It's Robertson. Alecia Marie Robertson."

Homer leaned forward and said indignantly, "Really, Brandon, this woman's sick joke has gone far enough, perhaps too far."

Brandon looked carefully at Homer and asked, "Do you know that name, Homer; Alecia Marie Robertson? You look as though it means something to you."

Homer swallowed profoundly and, with visible discomfort, said, "Why ah, yes, I certainly do recognize that name. Anyone who grew up during the '80s in Ashton would recognize that name. That's what makes this twisted gag so incredibly wrong. Poor Alecia was a young girl two grades behind me. We were friends. I knew her well as we had talked a lot back then before . . . well before it happened."

"Before what happened, Homer?" Brandon asked, leaning forward on his chair, "Can you tell us what happened?"

Homer took a deep breath and said, "Someone murdered that poor girl. One day her naked body was found in the bushes behind her home. She had been, well, sexually assaulted and beaten to death. None of us could forget that because our parents refused to let any of us go outside for the entire summer after her murder. They never caught her killer to the best of my knowledge, although to be honest, I haven't been back to Ashton in about thirty years."

Brandon hesitated for a moment, then asked, "But what could that possibly have to do with you? Why would this caller suggest you killed her?"

"It has nothing to do with me. That's why this horrible call is so despicable. To use such a horrendous and tragic event to make a crank call is deplorable! Brandon, I insist you hang up immediately!"

Brandon said, "Not just yet. Not until I give this caller a piece of my mind. Caller from Ashton, PA, are you still on the line?"

"Yes. I'm still here, and I'm still fifteen." The tone of the voice was flat and distant. "I'll always be fifteen because Homie killed me. Isn't that right, Homie?"

Brandon interrupted, "I'm sorry, ma'am, whoever you may be. I can't allow you to use the memory of a poor, slain child to further whatever sick and twisted agenda you're trying to force on my show and, more importantly, on my distinguished guest. So, I'm afraid I'm going to have to disconnect . . ."

He stopped mid-sentence, unable to finish his thought. He also couldn't disconnect the call. Brandon suddenly appeared to be unable to move a muscle. Homer heard the small ghostly voice coming over his headphones.

"I can't let you do that, Brandon. You're going to have to hold on for a bit. And Homie, you have to do something for me, and I would suggest you tell the truth and do it quickly. Tell the audience how you waited for me after school when I walked home. And tell them about all the bad things you did to me before you smashed my head in with that rock."

"I . . . I don't know what . . . you're lying caller. This caller is so, so wrong. Brandon, stop staring at me like a lunatic and disconnect the call."

However, Brandon wasn't able to do so. His eyes were bulging out of their sockets with terror at his helplessness. He seemed to be quivering from head to toe. Thin streams of drool trickled from the corners of his paralyzed mouth.

"He can't move Homie. I've seen to that. Just like I couldn't move when you sat on top of me and punched me until I promised not to scream. Why won't you talk about that, Homie? That's much more interesting than your stupid candy company anyway. Look closely at Brandon, Homie. He's not doing so well, is he?"

Homer was unable to say a word. He was stunned at the sudden comprehension that somehow, no matter how impossible it might seem, this person on the phone was that same girl, the same Alecia Marie Robertson he had killed more than three decades earlier. Homer looked again at Brandon, who appeared in the early stages of a seizure. He suspected the man wouldn't last much longer. Whatever power this ghost, this demonic version of the girl, had over the host, Homer was sure it would kill the man shortly.

"Why are you doing this, Alecia? What has Brandon ever done to you?"

"Him? Oh, nothing other than inviting you to the show, which, as it turns out, was a good thing. But then again, what did I ever do to you, Homie, to deserve what you did to me? I did nothing but tell you about my wild ideas for someday starting a gross candy company, and you stole them from me and took my life in the process. Now I want you to watch Brandon closely, Homie, because you're next. I want you to see what it's going to be like for you very soon."

"No, please, Alecia. Don't. Wha . . . what can I do to make you stop? The poor man is dying. Please just tell me before it's too late! The headphones were almost completely silent for a few moments, which seemed to amplify the sounds of Brandon's ragged breathing. Then she said, "Just tell the truth, Homie. Tell the people in the audience what you did to me."

"But, but . . ."

"Just do it, Homie. Or Brandon is going to die. Only you can save him and maybe yourself."

"Ok. Fine, fine, I'll confess," Homer said tearfully, "I did it. Ok? I assaulted and murdered Alecia Marie Robertson when I was a young man. I had to do it; I had no choice."

"Tell them why Homie. Tell them about my ideas and how you stole them."

"Yes, yes, you're right. The idea for the Revolting Candy Company was all yours. You thought of everything, all the candies, the names, the packaging, everything. I knew the ideas were incredible, and I wanted to claim them for myself. I killed you to steal your ideas and start my company. I raped you and bashed your skull in with a rock to made it look like some psycho had done it," Homer was weeping openly now.

"That's good, Homie. That's what I needed to hear. Doesn't that feel good? Now, look at Brandon, Homie. I'm letting him go. See, he's getting better already."

Homer looked with amazement as Brandon's quivering stopped, and his eyes once again began to focus. Homer was genuinely concerned for the host's wellbeing. "Are you all right, Brandon? Can you hear me?"

"Yes, yes, I'm fine," Brandon said. Then his face took on a look of anger as he spat, "But you're not going to be when the police get here."

"P . . . police? What are you saying? Why are the police coming?"

A voice came over the headphones. It was the girl, Alecia, but she suddenly sounded much older and more mature. "They're coming for you, Homer. They're coming because of the confession you've just made to a national radio audience of millions of listeners. You just admitted to murdering our sister."

"What are you talking about . . . our sister?"

"Brandon and my sister, Alecia."

Homer thought for a moment, then said, "Brandon? Brandon Robertson? And . . ."

"Anna. It's my sister Anna Jones, formerly Anna Robertson," Brandon said with disdain.

Homer said, "So your last name isn't Fisker?"

"It's my professional name, Homer. A lie, just like your entire life has been. You stole our sister's ideas, killed her, and made millions over the years. I suspected you for some time and couldn't wait to get you in here to find out the truth. But now that's over, Homer. The whole country now knows the truth, and soon so will the world. The police are on their way to take you into custody."

Homer began to regain his composure quickly and said calmly, "Well . . . Good luck with that, Brandon. You see, I, um, I knew who you were all the time. You didn't know I can be quite the actor myself. I was simply playing along with your gag to see how far you would take it, strictly for entertainment purposes, of course. My so-called confession was just a gag. Besides, you and your idiotic sister don't have a shred of proof to convict me. I confessed to nothing. It was simply radio theatrics. You might as well tell the police to stop wasting their time and not to bother coming here. Hell, I won't even need my high-priced team of attorneys to help me because you have nothing."

Brandon looked on in stunned silence, realizing Homer was right. He could hear his sister Anna quietly weeping owner the phone. She, too, knew their plan had failed.

He said, "But now I know the truth, Homer. And somehow, some-way, I'll get you for what you've done.

"Yes, well, good luck with that as well, Brandon."

Suddenly, from a darkened corner of the studio, Homer noticed a strange light appear. At first, it was in the form of a faintly glow-ing crimson orb; then, it slowly began to shape itself into something vaguely resembling the form of a woman.

Homer said, "Nice try, Brandon. How are you doing that little gimmick? Is it a trick of lighting, maybe a projected hologram? A very professional job, I might add. You still refuse to admit there's nothing you can do to me. You still won't give up the ghost. Hey, that was unintentionally funny."

Brandon sat staring with his mouth agape. As the glowing shape began to float ever closer to Homer, Brandon managed to stammer, "Nnnn no . . . I . . . I'm not doing that. I'm not doing anything."

"Yeah, right," Homer said as he stood to leave, "Well, I think this interview is over."

Brandon was determined not to let his sister's murderer escape, and he started to get up to intercept the candy baron, but he never got the chance. The glowing shape engulfed Homer, stopping him in his tracks as he looked disbelievingly out through the translucent blanket of sparkling particles.

For a moment, Homer was amazed not only by the beauty of the substance but by how serene he felt wrapped tightly in its essence. There was a familiarity emitting from the gelatinous substance, something familiar and comforting. That was, until the material tightened around him with a suffocating grasp, forcing the air out of his lungs. He tried desperately to breathe in and felt icy cold, thick liquid spill over his trembling lips, into his mouth, and down his throat. An instant later, his body began to dissolve, to liquidity, becoming one with the entity consuming him. Homer understood that after so many years, Alecia Robertson had returned for him at last.

HARVEST HOME

"Even so, Lord, quickly come, bring Thy final harvest home"
—Henry Alford 1844

The wind and rain battered the sides of the house as hail was suddenly added to the mix, clicking relentlessly against the windows, threatening to shatter them. The home sat at the end of a long, sparsely populated dirt and gravel road, the interior dimly lit by a few candles scattered throughout. The electricity had gone out several hours earlier.

"When do you suppose we'll get our power back?" Abby asked her husband.

"Not sure," Arthur replied. "I suppose nothing's gonna happen until this damned storm decides to relent."

"Yes, you're probably right. It's a shame the storm had to hit on Halloween night."

"Gonna mess things up for the kids this year for sure. I'll bet none of them will try to go out in this mess."

"I heard the township canceled trick-or-treating and rescheduled it for Friday night. Everything should be pretty well cleaned up by then."

"I certainly hope so," Arthur glanced toward the kitchen window and the darkness beyond, "There's gonna be a real mess to clean up for sure."

There was a loud banging at the front door, so loud the couple jumped in their seats.

"What the hell was that?"

Abby gave a nervous chuckle. "It's probably someone at the front door."

"I know it's somebody at the door! I was wondering why they're out in the middle of such a horrible storm."

"Well, why don't you see who it is?"

"I'm getting there. They'll just have to hold their horses. Galldang pests would probably bother me amid Armageddon!" He grabbed one of the emergency candles from the table and shuffled into the living room.

Arthur walked toward the front door, ceasing his grumbling when he had a strange feeling of dread. He'd never experienced any sensation like it and couldn't explain why he was having it now. Perhaps it was the blackout or the storm causing his unease. Whatever the reason, he put his hand on the doorknob and hesitated for just a moment. Then he turned the knob.

He lifted his candle and opened the door far enough to see out without the wind blowing his candle out. A tall figure in a long hooded black robe stood in the shadows. The roof did little to protect the man—at least Arthur assumed it was a man—from the gale-force winds and rain.

"What in Sam Hill do you want on such a God-forsaken night? Are ya daft, man?"

The figure stood in silence. Arthur tried to get a look at the stranger's face but couldn't.

"I asked, 'what do ya want?'" Arthur tried once more. "Well, the Hell with you, then. I ain't got no time for none of your Halloween pranks, young man. You best be on your way home."

Arthur slammed the door and began to grumble his way back to the kitchen.

"No good fer nothin' . . . ," he started, but the front door exploded, practically flying off its hinges. Arthur saw the hooded figure standing in the doorway. All the emergency candles flickered, and only the glass coverings on some of them kept the flame burning.

Arthur turned to face the intruder who floated across the threshold into the room. The door lifted and slammed behind him, seemingly on its own, dampening the sounds of the raging storm. An aura of crimson light showed around the stranger's long black robe, giving him the appearance of being illuminated from behind.

"Arthur? Who . . . what is that thing?" Abby was standing in the open doorway. "Something's not right about this, Arthur."

"Don't you worry none, Abby; he's just some young troublemaker who's about to have his butt handed to him." Arthur grabbed a poker from the fireplace and approached the intruder. "Look, you little wise ass. I don't know who you think you are or what you're trying to pull breaking into my home in that ridiculous Grim Reaper Halloween getup, but you're in for a very unpleasant surprise. I may be an old man, but I ain't no pushover. Back in the day, I fought my way through the jungles of Nam. Do you honestly think I'm afraid of the likes of you? Not likely! I was killing Charlie when your old man was still filling his diapers. Now, this is your last chance. Tell me what you want, and maybe I'll just call the cops, and if you're lucky, they might get here before I break too many of your bones."

For a moment, the creature did nothing, appearing to be contemplating what, if anything, to say. Then both Arthur and Abby felt a strange pulsing in their heads and heard a crackling, hissing sound, but not with their ears. It seemed to be deep in their skulls, in the very center of their brains. The sound began to change, to morph into some strange, at first, unintelligible form of speech. Abby thought, if a snake gained the power of speech, this might be how it would sound.

Then the words began to clarify, and both Arthur and Abby understood what the creature was communicating. "I have come for the harvest."

Abby said, "Harvest?"

"What the hell are you talking about, son?" Arthur questioned. "This ain't no farm. There ain't no harvest here."

The creature repeated, "I have come for the harvest. I have come to bring the harvest home."

The hooded figure slowly reached its skeletal hands to the hood, revealing a bleached white grinning skull. It began to glow red in the mysterious crimson light, and its eyes burned with firelight brighter than any candle in the room. It reached inside its long coat and withdrew a glimmering curved blade, a sickle on the end of a long wooden pole. The edge glowed with an impossible ruby luminescence.

Arthur raised his poker to strike, but before he even had a chance to swing, the creature's scythe sliced through the air so fast, Arthur never saw the movement. He screamed in pain as his ear was severed, landing with a sickening splat on the floor. Arthur dropped his poker and fell, one hand pressed to his skull as blood streamed through his fingers.

Inside Arthur's confused brain, he heard the serpentine voice of the stranger saying, "First the blade and then the ear."

Abby screamed from across the room and ran like a woman possessed toward the demon invader, swinging a knife. When she got within a few feet of the stranger, his sickle once again flashed through the air. Abby's arm was severed just below the elbow, and it, along with the blade, thudded harmlessly to the floor. She fell to her knees as her life's blood pumped from the wound.

In her mind, Abby heard the hissing invader say, "Free from sorrow, free from sin."

They struggled to maintain consciousness, but the creature swung the scythe back up, simultaneously decapitating them both in a single swipe. The couple's bodies flopped as their heads rolled into the dark corners on each side of the room.

For the first time, the demon spoke aloud to the now lifeless room, its raspy snake-like voice whispering, "I have come for the harvest. I have come to bring the harvest home. The harvest of souls."

SUB SANDWICHES

The two businessmen walked casually along the street, heading toward the area of the city known for its casual dining. The noonday sun warmed their faces making the spring day seem more like summer.

"I don't know what to do, Bob. This project has the potential of allowing us to sell many thousands of units. Right now, the factory is almost operating at full capacity. And with summer right around the corner, folks will be taking vacations, and others won't be willing to give up their weekends to work, even for overtime pay."

"Yeah, I know, Jim, but how the hell can we say no to such a great opportunity. And don't forget the high-profit margins we have on these components. It's a real money-maker. Besides, you know we always find some way to pull a rabbit out of our hats. I realize we must design, manufacture, assemble, and test the units, but I honestly think we can do it. Tell me. How many units do you think we can handle per month without risking our current customer orders? And be honest; don't be too conservative or over-ambitious either. I need to get a realistic feel here."

Jim thought for a moment, then said, "I honestly think we can push out another one to two hundred a month, but that's nowhere near the five to six hundred the customer is requesting."

Being the experienced salesman he was, Bob assured Jim saying, "Well, you leave that up to me. I think I can get the customer to accept, let's say, two hundred the first month with the right amount of persuasion. We can follow that with a fifty unit increase each month until we eventually find a way to get to four or five hundred per month by the end of the order."

"Wow! If you could pull that off, I honestly think we could find a way to make this work."

Before Jim finished his thoughts, a frantically running man slammed into him, practically knocking him to the ground. Jim managed to grab onto Bob for support. Lying on the ground, dressed in tattered rags that might have once been clothing, the wild man mumbled gibberish through his tongue-less mouth as he lay on the ground holding painfully onto his damaged leg.

"Don't worry gentlemen, we have him," a voice called from behind as two hulking uniformed men brandishing Tasers fell on the runner rendering him unconscious with fifty thousand volts of electricity.

"Thank you both so much," Jim said, startled.

"We're so sorry. This one got loose on us. Were either of you injured?" The concerned soldier asked.

Bob replied, "No, no, we're fine. Thanks. Just a bit shook up, is all."

"Damned freak, stinking subhuman," the other soldier replied, "I hate these bastards. Our bosses have us cut their tongues out so they can't shout and carry on, but I wish they'd let us hobble them so they couldn't run away."

With no further discussion, the two soldiers dragged the unconscious man away to a waiting recovery vehicle.

"Thank goodness you're all right, Jim. Do you realize what that creature could have done to you if he'd gotten a good grip on you?"

"Yeah, I do. Thank goodness the creature couldn't bite me. The handlers do still remove their teeth, don't they?"

"As far as I know, they do," Bob replied, "I believe they started doing that a few years ago after a few unpleasant and unfortunate incidents."

Jim said, "Yeah. Remember how it was back then, with these things roaming the streets, homeless, crazy, mumbling incoherently, and constantly bothering people?"

"Yep. And a good many of those people were dangerous as well," Bob said. Then he pointed up the street. "Hey, look, up ahead. What say we hit Gino's Deli for a couple of sub sandwiches? I realize you might not have much of an appetite after that encounter, but if you don't eat now, you'll be starving by this afternoon."

"Yeah, I suppose you're right. I should eat something."

As the pair approached the door to the deli, they heard the sound of a truck coming down the busy street. They saw it was a sizeable flat-bed style vehicle with a series of long open-barred crates stacked five high and a dozen deep all along both sides of the truck bed. As the truck got closer, they recognized one of the many inhabitants of the crates lying flat, staring out at the pedestrians with a dazed expression, twitching, spasmodically, every few seconds.

"Hey, isn't that the guy who almost knocked me down?" Jim said.

"Yeah, he won't be knocking anyone else down any time soon."

"You know Bob; even though I understand the necessity, I don't think I'll ever get used to seeing human beings caged in those crates."

"I know what you mean, but it's just something we have to accept. You can't think of those creatures as human beings either. They aren't the same as us, not by a long shot. It's how the government decided to handle a troublesome situation. Think about it this way; you love the taste of beef and chicken? But you have no desire to kill the animals yourself or go to a slaughterhouse to see the work in progress, right?"

Jim said, "Right, but who is it that makes the determination, you know, who decides who will go in the cages and who won't?"

"Why the government, of course, and their experts."

Looking around as if to make sure no one was listening, Jim asked, "But don't you ever wonder if maybe some normal people who might have pissed off the wrong people in charge could end up on one of those trucks?"

"No, I don't believe so, Jim. We have to trust our government to do what's right for us. They watch out for us and protect us. Without the government, where would we be?"

"Yeah. I suppose you're right. Still, it's the sort of thing that's open for abuse with the wrong people in charge, don't you think?"

"No, not really, Jim. I'm sure there are a series of checks and balances in the process to make sure nothing goes wrong. Remember when it all first was proposed by the government so many years ago? It was a bit weird for those of us who were already adults, but now a generation later, our kids just accept it. To them, it's perfectly normal."

"I suppose so. But those trucks look like the old chicken trucks from back when we were kids. The one that they used to haul hundreds of chickens to slaughter."

"Yeah, I know. But that was a different time and a whole different situation. I wonder, where do you suppose those trucks are going? Do you think they're heading off to the camps, or maybe they're going for processing?"

Jim thought for a moment, then said, "Don't know, and I suppose I shouldn't care. I prefer not to think about it anymore. Let's go get our subs."

The pair entered the deli, smelling the unique aromas of cooking meat. Taking their place in line, Jim looked behind the counter where a large, browned slab was cooking, rotating on a spit over an open gas flame—wielding a gleaming carving knife, one of the butchers cut off a thin slice just behind the neck stump where its head used to be.

"Wow, it smells incredible in here. I think I'm getting my appetite back," Jim said.

Bob agreed, "Yeah, me too."

They saw the sign hanging overhead as they approached the counter and seemed to pay it little interest. The sign read, "Subhuman sandwiches. The best in town."

NIGHTMARE SHADOWS

It is absolutely necessary, for the peace and safety of mankind,
that some of earth's dark, dead corners and unplumbed depths be
left alone; lest sleeping abnormalities wake to resurgent life, and
blasphemously surviving nightmares squirm and splash out of their
black lairs to newer and wider conquests.

—H. P. LOVECRAFT

The room was in almost complete darkness. Eric opened his eyes with
a start, realizing he couldn't move a single muscle in his body. He tried
to speak but couldn't. However, he could hear, feel and smell. His
sinuses filled with a scent of something slightly damp and earthy like
that of rotting forest vegetation. His heartbeat quickened as he felt
panic set in.

A thin shaft of moonlight crept in under the window blinds. Eric's
stomach clenched with fear as he suddenly became aware of another
presence in the room with him. He saw a shadow moving in a corner
then sensed it moving further into his field of vision. Staring in paralytic
horror, he saw the thing's eyes glow like two fires in the blackness. He
heard the shadow creature whispering his name in a hissing serpentine
voice calling, "Eerrriccc. . . ."

A cold chill crept down his back. He imagined the shadow creature
dragging one of its icy fingers down his spine. Eric wanted to scream,

lash out, and pull his hair from his skull in frustrating madness like a raving lunatic. Anything would be preferable to the slow, demeaning torture carried out by this unseen demon of the dark.

The blaring ring of his alarm clock woke Eric with heart-pounding shock. He sat up in bed, throwing his legs over the side, and stared into the corner of the room where he had seen the shadow creature originate. For the briefest moment, he thought he still saw the dark form hiding in the shadows, but the image quickly faded. He was relieved to find the morning had come, and he was able to move once again.

After completing his morning rituals and eating a good breakfast, Eric took a cup of coffee and headed to the old manual typewriter to work on his latest book. He knew his word processor would be more efficient, but this week was about leaving the trappings of modern technology behind. His book was about an affliction known as Sleep Paralysis or SP. After a significant amount of research, he had begun writing a book on the subject. Little had he realized when he took on the project that an unpleasant side effect of his writing would be his suffering from attacks of SP.

As a twenty-five-year-old, it was hard for Eric to imagine that in this summer of 1997, he would find himself so stressed and plagued by the frantic pace of his life. It had become so intense that his psychiatrist recommended he spend a week or so away in this semi-isolated cottage by a lake. There he would be able to work on his book in peace and solitude. Although a bit small with no TV, cell, or internet service, the cottage was quite lovely and had a spectacular view of the sparkling lake beyond. It also had a landline telephone attached to an answering machine for emergencies. He listened to the unfamiliar sounds of the woodlands coming in through the front screen door; birds chirping, leaves rustling in the breeze, water gently lapping against the shore below. Yes, this place indeed was just what the doctor ordered.

By mid-morning, Eric decided to take a break. He sat on the edge of the boat dock with his feet dangling over the side just above the lake. The place was deserted, which was all right with him. The lake's mirror-like surface glistened in the evening sunlight, and Eric was amazed by how still and quiet the water was. He lay back on the dock, looking up at the clear, blue sky. He closed his eyes to relax for just a moment and listen to more of the calming sounds of nature around him.

Minutes later, he heard a slight splashing sound, and sitting up, Eric noticed a rippling on the surface just below his feet. The air around him seemed to have taken on a foul, fishy scent. He looked down, expecting to see a fish or perhaps a frog in the water but instead saw something he couldn't believe.

From below the surface, two black skeletal arms began to arise. Before Eric had a chance to react, the hands grabbed tightly around his ankles and began to pull him down. Eric fought to stay on the dock, but it had suddenly somehow become slick with moisture, and he couldn't keep from slipping. Sliding off the wooden planking, Eric could see the top of a black skull sticking up out of the water, its hollow eye sockets blazing with crimson light. He heard it hissing his name as the creature pulled him down into the water. "Eerrrricccc!"

Eric opened his eyes with a start, realizing he must have fallen asleep. He was still lying on his back on the dock, although his dangling legs had grown numb and not from sleep paralysis. His numbness had been from lack of blood circulation. He suddenly realized just how lucky he was he hadn't fallen into the water below, especially with no one around to help him. The memory of his nightmare had begun to fade as such things often do. The sun was setting over the western end of the lake.

Upon returning to the cottage, Eric saw the message light on the answering machine was blinking with a number "1," indicating he had a message waiting. Eric pressed the PLAY button.

"Hey, Eric, it's Walter," Eric's editor's voice said, "Give me a call as soon as you get this. Don't worry about the time, just call. You know the number."

Eric picked up the receiver and dialed the number from memory. After two rings, Walter answered. "Yello," he said with his typical way-too-pleasant voice.

"Walter, it's Eric returning your call. What's up?"

"Hey, Eric, nothing's up. I just wanted to check up on you and see how things are going out there in the wilderness."

"Going fine for the most part. This place is great and very relaxing. It's helping me make great progress on the book."

"That great to hear," Walter hesitated for a moment then asked, "What about . . . you know, the dreams and the other stuff? Are you still having SP attacks?"

"Well, yeah, I suppose I am. Had one last night, but I'm hoping after a few more days up here, they'll lessen and maybe stop altogether."

"I certainly hope so. This getaway is what Dr. Moravian recommended, so I would think it should help."

"I'm sure it will, Walter. Is there anything else?"

"Nah, that's all. I just wanted to check on my up-and-coming best-selling author."

"Ok, well then, thanks for checking, and I'll talk to you again maybe tomorrow. Bye, Walter."

"Later, Eric."

After preparing and eating his dinner, Eric sat on a comfortable recliner in the living room and began to read through what he had written so far, making notes and corrections where required. Realizing he was starting to fall asleep once more, Eric put down the book and went to bed. He fluffed his pillow, crawled under the covers, and without his typical anxiety, fell immediately into a deep and restful sleep.

Several hours later, Eric's eyes flew open. His bedroom was in almost complete darkness, save for some minimal moonlight coming through a crack in the curtains. He could smell a dank, musty scent in the air. Suddenly the light was interrupted by a black shadow appearing to move quickly across its path. Eric tried to sit up but realized he couldn't move, understanding he was suffering from another sleep paralysis attack. He did his best to remain calm, as Dr. Moravian has suggested, hoping to shorten the duration of the attack.

Eric heard high-pitched heavy breathing as once again the shadow moved across the light from the slim opening in the heavy curtains. Then the breathing became louder as if whoever or whatever made the sound moved ever closer to him. As he lay still, feeling his ability to remain calm quickly diminishing, Eric heard a soft, hissing whisper close to his ear.

"Eerrricc," the snake-like voice spat, "Sssurely you didn't think you could get away from us that easssssily did you, Eerrriccc?"

Eric couldn't cry out in his paralytic state. He realized this was the first time the horrid creatures had ever spoken to him more than to call his name. Eric understood this attack had suddenly become much more severe. As the shadow got ever closer, Eric could feel the icy chill surrounding the thing. Despite his inability to move, he began to shiver involuntarily. His ear felt like someone had opened up a freezer door next to him as icy tendrils seemed to slither deep into his ear canal and creep down the side of his throat.

The voice whispered, "You want to write a book about us, Eerrriccc? Sssssseriously? About me? About my friendsssss? What are you going to sssssay about us, Eerrriccc? Are you going to sssssay we're not real, just figments of imagination? Issss that what you're going to sssssay about us, Eerrrriccc?"

Eric began to feel the side of his face and throat grow numb from the frigid drop in temperature. He was helpless to do anything to stop the spreading cold.

"Haha, nicsssse try my foolisssssh friend. You ssssshould have known I could never permit that sssssort of thing, even if it'sss nothing more than lines in a book no one will read. I sssimply cannot allow you to sssssspoil my fun. Or that of my friendssss either."

Eric could hear quiet whispering from all around the room. It was as if there were more than a dozen creatures similar to the first. As he lay paralyzed, the combined hissing moved closer as the room temperature began to plummet even further.

"We were hoping to keep our little game going on for a long time to come, Eerriccc, but sssssadly you have left us no choice. We're going to have to take you now and make you one of ussss. I think you alwayssss ssssuspected that ssssooner or later we would have to do that."

An icy chill raced throughout Eric's body as, one by one, the shadow creatures poked him, feeling like dozens of icy knives were penetrating his flesh. The agony was initially incredible until, one by one, each stabbed area went numb. He suddenly realized it wouldn't matter soon if he could move or not as he felt far too cold to move anyway.

Just when Eric was sure he couldn't possibly get any colder, the subzero chill passed deep inside him, turning his insides to ice. He could feel his heart gradually slowing down inside his chest, each thump becoming slower and softer with every strenuous beat.

His eyes began to droop as he felt the overpowering need to just go to sleep. But Eric knew once he closed his eyes, he would never open them again. He imagined his blood slowing its journey through his body. Then everything came to a final stop.

When Eric opened his eyes, the room was still dark, but he was surprised to find he could see clearly in the blackness. He felt like he was floating around the room high in the air. Then Eric looked down and saw his body lying on the bed below him. He immediately understood it was a corpse. This realization should have filled him with dread, but for some reason, it didn't. Through the darkness, he looked around and saw more than a dozen smoky black shapeless figures floating about the room with him. He lifted what he thought of as his hand and saw what looked like a smoky distorted representation of what a hand might have once been.

As the creatures floated toward him, Eric was no longer afraid. He immediately sensed a kinship with them. He also had an understanding that he and his newfound family had to leave this place. Somewhere out there in the night, someone was about to have an attack of sleep paralysis, and Eric, with his new brotherhood, would have to be on hand to do their part.

FACES IN A CROWD

There are times when the fabric separating the world we think of as usual and that which we consider impossible becomes pulled so tightly; stretched so thin, things from the realm of the unreal ooze over into our world. Think of a liquid being fed through a cheesecloth filtering out impurities. As the cloth becomes worn or stretched too thin, the guarantee of purity becomes null and void as imperfections seep into what was supposed to be a clean solution. Whenever this occurs, there are consequences. There are often grave and unpredictable consequences for those innocents caught in the crossfire.

Seth Rhinebeck took advantage of the mild fall day by spending his lunch hour sitting on a bench in the park a stone's throw from his office. Two concrete side pieces with wooden slats for a seat and back made up the bench. He had probably sat on this particular bench more times than he could remember, so often that some of the pigeons had come to anticipate his arrival. They waited patiently for Seth to finish his sandwich. The birds knew he would throw them crusts eventually.

As he sat eating, Seth looked up and saw someone strolling casually toward him. There was nothing out of the ordinary about this. People had been walking back and forth in front of him for the past fifteen minutes. Seth had been paying little if any attention to the walker. Yet there was something about this one that suddenly caught his eye, something familiar. Perhaps it was the man's build or the way he carried himself. Maybe it was his walk or his manner of dress. He wore a dark grey suit, with a white shirt and black tie. He had shiny black shoes and a Fedora that sat atop his head at a jaunty angle. The entire ensemble seemed somehow antiquated, perhaps several decades out of fashion.

The gentleman didn't appear to be paying any particular attention to him, that was until he came to a stop in front of Seth and looked directly at him. The man's face was blank, void of expression, yet in those cold unemotional eyes, Seth saw something he recognized.

"That's Bill Dewar," Seth thought. Bill had been his co-worker for a time many years earlier at his first job. The company had hired Seth straight out of college. At that time, old Bill was a year from retirement. Strange as it might seem, Bill looked the same as he had the last time Seth had seen him.

Seth started to raise his hand to wave to Bill when he realized, "Wow, I haven't seen Bill since . . ." Then the thought hit him like a baseball bat to the face. ". . . since his funeral."

Bill had died a little over six months after Seth had started with the company. As he recalled, the man had suffered a stroke and died two days later. The two weren't what Seth would consider friends; however, they had been polite, cordial, and professional coworkers. As such, Seth had attended the man's burial services.

Seth pulled his arm down and looked away, realizing he had almost waved to a total stranger, mistaking him for a former acquaintance now more than twenty years in his grave. The stranger turned away and continued to walk along, blending in with the rest of the crowd.

Seth said to himself, "It must all be a coincidence; just a trick of the light is all. I'm certain that has to be the case."

Yet, somewhere deep in the illogical part of Seth's mind, a nearly silent voice whispered, "You can believe, whatever you wish, Seth old boy. Listen to your logical self if you choose, but we know the truth here. We've seen through your eyes, and like it or not, we know."

Seth chose to ignore the voice and write it off as nothing more than his childhood imagination, trying to reassert itself in adulthood as it often did at the most inopportune times. Seth stood, threw the crusts of his sandwich to the pigeons, and began walking back to his office.

Typically, Seth kept his head down when he walked, avoiding eye contact with his fellow citizens. He preferred to enjoy being alone with his thoughts. However, today Seth was observing the faces and expressions of all the people coming his way. He suspected the strange encounter with the Bill Dewar lookalike must have had something to do with it.

He observed a sea of faces of all ages, genders as well as numerous ethnic persuasions. Each of them was strolling along, paying no attention to Seth or to anyone else for that matter. Those in couples or small groups laughed and chatted among themselves, while most singles seemed mesmerized, staring intently into their smartphones. Seth had left his cell phone back on his desk, preferring to be unreachable while on his break. Then he saw something that didn't fit with the rest of the picture.

In the distance, Seth noticed a woman ambling, wearing a long, lightweight beige raincoat and a floral scarf around her head. He recalled the name of such a scarf from his childhood growing up in Pennsylvania's ethnically diverse anthracite region. People referred to the scarf as a *babushka*, which Seth believed originated with Polish immigrants. He hadn't seen anyone wearing one of those scarves in decades.

The woman looked directly at him as she walked. There was a cold unemotional quality to the woman's expression that seemed frighteningly like the man he had seen earlier. And there was something else about this woman. He couldn't recall her name, but he had seen her face somewhere before in his life; perhaps she was a teacher from his grammar school days. Yes, that seemed right. But how could she now look the same as she had back then, and why was she staring at him in such a horrible way?

Seth stopped walking, forced his eyes away from the almost hypnotic gaze of the woman, and looked back at the oncoming crowd. There, off to the right, he saw another man staring at him with that same dead-eyed expression. Wasn't that Joe the barber Seth had gone to many years ago? Then he saw another person he thought he recognized, then another. Before he knew it, Seth realized everyone slowly walking toward him had that same strange emotionless expression, that same bizarre familiarity, and they were all staring directly at him.

He looked around, trying to determine what happened to the rest of what he thought of as ordinary people. They all appeared to have gone. There was no one in sight save for this mass of strange beings slowly surrounding him and silently staring at him. Where had everyone gone?

"What, what do you want with me?" He asked the crowd. There was no response from the onlookers as they all took a step closer.

He begged, "Please, just tell me why you're here. Why don't you just go away and leave me alone?" They all took another synchronized step forward, then another, then another. Seth began to frantically look from face to face hoping against hope to find a way out of this horrible situation. Over to the left, he saw a teenage boy. It was Bobby Meister, a boy from his high school who died unexpectedly of an aneurysm. To the right, he saw Emma Johns, his church's organist; or at least she had been before she died in that house fire.

Visages of long-dead people surrounded him. Most he didn't remember well, but all of them had come wanting something from him. As the circle of the dead closed in upon Seth, they raised their arms to touch him and pull him into their icy embrace. Their touch was unlike anything Seth had ever felt before. As the dozens of hands touched him, Seth felt himself drifting away, and he could do nothing to stop the sensation.

"Hey, somebody call 911!" The voice of a young man shouted, "We have a man down over here!"

"What happened?" someone else asked.

He replied, "I have no idea. One minute this guy was walking along minding his business, then the next thing I know, he was screaming about dead people, and then he collapsed into a heap."

"Dead people? Maybe the guy's on drugs," one person said.

Another suggested, "Or maybe he's off his meds."

The young man bent down and put his fingers against Seth's throat, unable to find a pulse. He said, "Well, whatever his story might be, this dude's a goner."

"You mean he's dead?"

"Oh yeah, he's gone. El dead a Mundo."

Near the back of the crowd, unseen by onlookers, two men walked casually away from the group. One was dressed in an old out-of-date suit and a fedora, while the other wore more modern clothing. As they walked away silently together, they were joined by several other slow-moving people, all heading in the same direction. They were unseen by anyone else as they made their way to another encounter with someone else who would see their faces in a crowd.

HAERID'S DEAL

Author's note: This is the short story version of a radio play script I wrote for the Blood Noir podcast. It is a continuation of the radio play, The Line Went Dead, *written by Mark Slade. He asked me to pick up where his story left off and see what happened. Not to worry, you can enjoy this even if you didn't read it.*

A gentle rain fell on that dark July night as Freddy Madison wandered down the city street, his slow, steady footsteps audible on the wet pavement. He had a lot on his mind that evening. Freddy was the host and creator of the Conspiracy X radio program. It was a late-night program that delved into almost every sort of conspiracy theory imaginable and had a devoted following of like-minded fans.

"I can hardly believe what happened.," he thought to himself, "And to think it occurred right in the middle of my radio broadcast too."

Freddy had received a call from a female fan which at first seemed crackly, garbled, and unintelligible until the line cleared, and the real trouble started.

Freddy thought, "Like it wasn't bad enough I heard the woman apparently being murdered over the telephone, but then to later learn that the same woman, Beryl Nelson, had been murdered by her husband Daniel way back on December 30th, 1973."

Although the event was the sort of thing a program like his knew would be excellent live radio, the entire event had Freddy frazzled. He knew it was a scam since dead people don't typically call radio programs, but it sounded so real, so authentic it still managed to disturb him.

"Whoever's idea it was, they got me good," Freddy thought. "I had even called the police after it happened, thinking it was the real deal. I can't believe the cops acted like I was the one who was making a crank call. They even threatened to arrest me for filing a false report."

Freddy was glad the cops had not arrested him since he was not well-liked among the radio station managers. If his program hadn't brought in the superior ratings, it did; management would have tossed his sorry butt out the door long ago. Ratings or not, there would be no way the station would back him if the cops hauled him away. They'd likely find some way to turn the incident into a publicity bonanza for the station and have a replacement sitting in his chair within a day.

"And what was all that crap she was spouting about her father being torn apart by a demon named Haerid?"

Deep in thought about the disturbing call, Freddy stepped off the curb onto the street without paying attention to where he was going. Suddenly he was startled back to reality by the ear-splitting sound of a blaring car horn as a black sedan sped by, its driver waving his fist and shouting. "Get back on the sidewalk, you damned lunatic! Are you drunk or what?"

"Jesus! He almost ran me down," Freddy said to himself, suddenly realizing water saturated his pant legs. The speeding car had hit a nearby puddle and splashed him. "That was a close one. I'd better watch where I'm going."

Up ahead, he heard lots of people talking and music playing as a couple entered a neighborhood bar. Freddy decided this might be just what he needed to get himself back under control.

"Maybe I better get off the street for a while and sort all of this out. Yes, Freddy, my boy, I think it's time you join that crowd in the bar over there for an adult beverage, or maybe several. Besides, my two-am shift at the station doesn't start for a few hours, so what the hell."

Inside, the bar, packed to capacity, lots of people were speaking loudly, and the jukebox was playing classic rock. Freddy approached the bar and ordered his favorite concoction. "Gimmie a whiskey and soda and make it a double."

Freddy relaxed on his barstool and began to think again about the bizarre phone call. The woman who called said her father had ties to an urban legend from Copper Creek in Saint Louis. The story said that an eighteen-year-old young man and his girlfriend were making love in the grass back in 1939 when supposedly a demon appeared in a flash of light, killing and dismembering the boy. The girl managed to escape unharmed and reported the incident. She had become pregnant, and the result of that encounter had been a daughter, Beryl Nelson.

The caller, who claimed to be the same late Beryl Nelson, said the demon's name was Haerid, and after pulling her father's soul into the depths of Hell, he made some sort of deal with him. Freddy had no idea how the yet unborn daughter of the murdered teenager could have any knowledge of such a deal taking place; however, that was what she claimed. She had also said the demon Haerid would provide a list of people whose souls he wanted to acquire, and it was up to the decedents of her father to assure he got those souls listed.

Freddy ordered another drink and was sitting quietly at the bar deep in thought when he heard a voice next to him saying, "Hey there."

He turned and saw a beautiful woman standing next to him. She looked too gorgeous to exist so pretty that Freddy was struck dumb for a moment. He knew precisely what he'd like to do with a woman this good-looking. When he finally got his voice back, he decided to turn on all the charm he could muster.

"Hey there yourself, lovely lady. I'm Freddy Madison. What, may I ask yours is?"

The woman smiled at him, knowing what he was thinking, and replied, "I'm Gina. Gina Rogers."

Freddy turned on his thousand-dollar smile and said, "Well, it's terrific to meet you, Gina Rogers. Can I buy you a drink?"

"Sure, what are you drinking?"

"I'm having whiskey and soda, a double. Well, since this one is my second, I suppose it's a four-ple."

Gina chuckled and said, "You're funny, Freddy. A double sounds a bit strong for me; make mine a single."

Freddy turned to the bartender and ordered a drink for Gina. She took a healthy sip and seemed to sigh with pleasure, "Oh wow, that really hits the spot."

"Yeah. I agree," Freddy said, then he asked, "Say, I don't believe I've ever seen you in here before. Do you live around here, or are you just visiting our fair city?"

She replied, "I'm staying over at the Hyatt. I'm just in for the weekend, from Saint Louis."

Freddy hesitated, caught a bit off guard by the mention of Saint Louis, "Um, Saint Louis, you say. Funny, I was just thinking about Saint Louis.

"You were? I didn't think anyone thought about Saint Louis."

"Well, I was thinking about an urban legend known around that area, about Copper Creek Red. Did you ever hear that one?"

She seemed to hesitate for a moment, then said, "Oh yes. Everybody in Saint Louis knows about that story."

"Well," Freddy began to explain, "I'm a local radio DJ, and I have this program called *Conspiracy X*."

"A radio personality. Wow, I'm impressed."

Freddy was sure the mention of his radio show just sealed the deal with the woman as it always did. He noticed he was starting to feel the effects of his second drink, which tended to build his confidence and stimulate his nether regions. Feigning humility, he said, "You don't have to be. It's just a job, you know. Anyway, a few nights ago, this woman called into the radio show claiming to be the daughter of the teenager who was the victim of that story."

Gina said, "Daughter? That would have to be Beryl Nelson."

Surprised, Freddy asked, "You know about Beryl Nelson?"

"Sure, that name is sort of an urban legend as well. I assume you know she was murdered by her husband Daniel back in the '70s?"

"Yeah, so I heard, Gina. The actual year was 1973.

"1973 sounds right to me. So, the caller couldn't possibly be her. It had to be a crank call."

"Yeah, that's what I thought as well. But why would someone call me pretending to be Beryl and go through the trouble of acting out her murder on my show?"

"I don't know, Freddy; maybe she did it to get some attention. You know people can be weird."

"Yeah, I suppose you're right. So, Gina, do you know about the demonic aspect of the story as well?

"Yeah, I do. The demon supposedly had a list of souls he wanted to claim."

"That's what I heard as well. The demon's name was Haerid, so I've heard.

"Yeah, Haerid, that's right," Gina agreed.

Gina took another long sip of her drink, and Freddy's confidence continued to grow. If he could just loosen her up a little more, he'd close this deal. Then to his surprise, she turned to him and said, "So what time does your show start?"

He replied, "It starts in about three hours. Why do you ask?"

She paused for a moment then said, "So you have time then?"

"Time? Time for what?"

"Time to walk me back to my hotel and maybe come upstairs with me."

Freddy was flabbergasted. He couldn't believe his luck. Freddy was going to score with this gorgeous woman, and right before his show. As upset and distracted as he had been earlier, things were looking up for him this night. This night could prove to be the best he ever had. He slapped some dollars down on the bar and said, "Sounds like a plan to me."

Gina held up her right hand in a stop gesture and said, "Now wait a second here, lover boy. I didn't get to finish my drink yet."

She quickly downed the remainder of her drink as Freddy leaned over and whispered in her ear with a deep husky voice, "There you go, now let's get out of here."

The couple was walking down the street much too slowly for Freddy's taste. He was a man on a mission, but the lady in question forced him to stroll. He supposed this was all part of how she liked things done, so if he needed to play along to win the grand prize, so be it.

Gina took his hand and said, "Thank goodness the rain has stopped. It'll make the walk to the hotel easier."

"Yes, it certainly will. By the way, Gina, what brings you to our city, business or pleasure?"

"Originally, it was for business, but now it looks like it'll be for pleasure," she chuckled and gave him a knowing, enticing look.

As his face flushed with heat, Freddy agreed, "You've got that right."

They continued to walk hand in hand at Gina's painfully slow pace when she asked, "So your radio station; is it nearby?"

Freddy was starting to feel the effects of his drink now and, unknowing, was becoming much chattier than he would have preferred to be, "Actually, yes, it is. It's just up the street from your hotel. 105 Denver Boulevard, Suite 10E is where we call home."

Gina then asked Freddy a question that should have caused some alarms to go off. However, in his state of intoxication, he seemed not to notice. "Interesting. Is Walter Heller still the evening station manager there?"

Hearing the familiar name, Freddy went off on a rambling monologue, "Why, yes, he is. And I'll tell you something; he doesn't like me very much. He hates my guts and hates the idea of me coming onto his shift. That was until I started getting him great ratings. Now he still hates my guts, but he likes the ratings. Right now, he's probably sitting up there in his office on the 10th floor thinking of new ways to make my life miserable."

Then it suddenly hit him that Gina, a supposed stranger in town, had asked about Walter by name, "Hey . . . hey wait a minute. How do you know Walter?"

Gina smiled at him and said, "I don't know him. Not really. It's just that I have his name on this list." She reached in her purse and pulled out a piece of crimson paper with gold leaf writing on it. It appeared to be some sort of list.

He asked with a quavering voice, "What sort of list is that?"

She said, "The list I got from Haerid, the demon. You know, it's a newer version of a similar list he gave to my grandfather in Hell, which then passed on to my grandmother. Eventually, Haerid gave one to my mother, Beryl, and now he gave one to me. It's all part of the deal."

Freddy was starting to feel dizzy and uncertain on his feet. He asked with a voice that was becoming thick, "The deal? What deal?"

Gina smiled and explained, "You know, Haerid's deal; the deal he made with my grandfather after killing him. Now two generations later, our family is still carrying out the terms of that original deal. Some folks might call it a curse, but we like to think of it as a family responsibility. You see, we bring Haerid the souls he chooses and puts on the list. Then when we eventually die, our souls get a high-level place of honor in Hell."

Freddy couldn't believe what Gina was saying. He wasn't even sure if he heard what he had. Then he had a sudden realization, "S . . . so it was . . . was you who called my program the other night pretending to be your murdered mother."

Gina smiled and said, "Of course it was me, silly. Dead people don't call radio stations."

"And you . . . you're here for Walter?"

"Yep, you bet. And thanks to your information, I'll be taking Walter tonight."

After a moment of confused thought, Freddy asked, "I don't care what happens to Walter but . . . but . . . w . . . what about me?"

"You? Don't worry, Freddy. Nothing's gonna happen to you. You're not on the list."

He asked, "But I know about it now. I know about you and Haerid."

"So what, Freddy, lots of people know about the list. Remember it's an urban legend?"

"But I know it's real now."

Gina said, "That's not a problem. You can tell anybody you want. You can even talk about it on your radio program if you'd like. No one will believe it any more than they believe any of the crap you talk about on your program. *Conspiracy X*? Seriously? What a lame name. The only people who might believe you are your wacko fans, and no one cares what they believe."

Gina pointed her hand in Freddy's direction and began issuing some sort of almost silent chant while wiggling her fingers at him.

"Hey, what . . . what's that you're doing? Whoa, I'm feeling dizzy."

Within seconds, Freddy collapsed to the ground in a slumbering heap, appearing to onlookers like just another reveler who had too much to drink that night.

Gina said, "Good night, Freddy. By the time you wake up, I'll be long gone. And so will Walter Heller. Well, at least you've got some new material for your show. Enjoy."

WHAT IS A MAN?

"The good man is the friend of all living things."
—MAHATMA GANDHI

"It is not death that a man should fear, but he should
fear never beginning to live."
—MARCUS AURELIUS

"Death may be the greatest of all human blessings."
—SOCRATES

The massive creature sat silently, hunched on the chill, damp cave floor. The beast listened to the hypnotic drip, drip, dripping of water somewhere deep in the blackness, painstaking forming stalactites and stalagmites as it had done for millions of years before. He could hear the steady thump, thump, thumping of his own oversized heart sounding like the rhythmic beating of tribal drums echoing in his mind as the water reverberated in the near silence of the cavern.

Lining the walls surrounding him were bookshelves reaching ten feet tall, overflowing with thousands of volumes containing the most significant writings in human history. Wooden creates and skids held stacks upon stacks of even more books; classic fiction, historical accounts, religious essays, and scientific journals. He had read them all, most more than once. He had acquired them over many years, and they were among his most prized possessions.

In the darkness of a nearby alcove, an old-fashioned gramophone complete with hand crank stood ready for use along with stacks of hundreds of classic orchestral albums. When not reading, the creature loved to listen to music. On any available wall space remaining in the cavern, not occupied by bookshelves, priceless works of art by some great masters and ancient tapestries hung for his viewing pleasure.

Near his feet, a small collection of hot coals burned, the remnants of his former fire. He would rebuild the fire again soon, not for heat but for light so that he might read throughout the night. Presently, his massive muscular arms rested on his knees, allowing his shovel-sized hands to dangle down over tree-trunk-like legs. His bucket-sized head hung low as his chin rested on his barrel chest below massive shoulders more than five feet across. Although the cave was quite cold, the chilly temperatures never bothered him.

The monstrous hulking creature might appear to have been sleeping to an uninformed onlooker, but he was not. He never slept because he didn't need to sleep. He hadn't slept in years, perhaps decades. This particular restive position was the closest he ever came to sleeping. He thought of it as his thinking pose, and although his frightening physical appearance might suggest otherwise, the thinking was what he enjoyed doing most.

He suddenly sat bolt upright, his eyes glowing like the embers in his fire. He remained motionless now, silent in the shadows, carefully listening to the shuffling noise coming from the front of the cave near the entrance. He immediately recognized the familiar gate he had heard so many times before. It was another one of those wretched things; the dead ones. Somehow one of the creatures must have inadvertently found its way into his cave. Adam could feel his anger growing. How dare this abomination enter his home! He would be sure to guarantee this encounter would not end well for the intruder.

Adam wondered how many of those mindless shambling creatures remained in the world. Hundreds of them? Perhaps thousands? Possibly millions? He suspected millions might be an accurate assumption from a national perspective, but maybe only a few hundred locally. Humankind had done an exemplary job of eradicating the monsters over the past twelve years.

The shambling creature slowly made its way across the cave and into the minimal light cast by the dwindling fire. Adam studied the thing carefully. It appeared to have once been a male, but decomposition had taken its toll, which made distinguishing its gender almost impossible. Its clothing was in tatters, and it made that same low guttural growl they all made. The vile stench coming off the unholy beast was beyond appalling. This one had been decomposing for quite some time.

Adam knew well what these undead creatures, these zombies did whenever they encountered living humans. They ripped their victims to pieces, devouring their flesh and innards. He fumed at the very notion of one of these wretched things tromping about in his home, his anger continuing to grow.

The undead monster advanced, stumbling about the cave, apparently unaware of his presence. Adam stood and rose to his full height of eight feet, yet still, the creature ignored him. Then again, they always ignored him. It seemed like he was invisible to them. This phenomenon, too, caused him incredible frustration. Perhaps for personal reasons, he felt it better not to consider why he was so angry.

He bellowed in a booming angry voice, "Do you not see me, you disgusting pile of rotting meat? Here I am, standing right before you. Am I not made of human flesh and blood? Do you not wish to partake of my body, you revolting spawn of Hell?"

The zombie stood and stared, not so much at Adam as through him. It was like the zombie was confused, uncertain as to what his next move should be. Adam believed the creature could hear him shouting but, for whatever reason, couldn't sense him. He had tried this experiment on the undead countless times with the same futile results, and it was becoming maddening. Who was it who had said the definition of insanity was repeating the same thing over and over but expecting different results? Adam couldn't recall, but the recollection was making him question his sanity.

A low moan came from the zombie's throat, sounding not so much threatening as bewildered. It started to turn away. With one mighty swipe of his muscular arm, Adam severed the creature's head from its body, sending the skull flying across the cave and slamming into a wall with a sickening crack. The body thudded to the cave floor. He wasn't sure exactly why separating the head from the body or why, by simply making the brain inactive, killed the creatures; he just knew it worked.

He had accidentally discovered this fact many years earlier, more out of frustration than through any scientific process. He has come upon one of the monsters in the forest. It was a huge male, not as large as himself but still quite threatening in appearance. At that time, Adam was not only unaware the dead were reanimating, he also didn't know that they paid him no mind. He thought the creature was a living, breathing man and, therefore, a potential enemy. His natural assumption was to believe the monster would try to attack him. After all, anyone coming upon him his entire life would attack first and ask questions later.

Reaching out, Adam had grabbed onto the thing's left arm and pulled it from the socket. To his shock, no blood spurted from the stump, only a slight trickle of some viscous, puss-like fluid leaked out. The creature didn't seem even to notice his injury. Eager to end the encounter, Adam thrust his long arm outward toward his opponent's chest, penetrating his flesh with surprising ease and pulling out what he assumed would be his attacker's still-beating heart.

To his dismay, Adam held a dead gray, bloodless thing that teamed with maggots in its advanced stage of decomposition. And still, the creature stood. It looked down at the hole in its chest for a moment, then let out a deep growing sound. Frustrated and unsure what to do next, Adam bent down, retrieved the severed arm, then swinging it like a war club, he struck the creature's head. Its spinal column snapped with an audible crack, causing it to fall to the ground. He test-kicked the mass of flesh, and it remained inanimate. He made a mental note that if he ever came upon a creature such as this again, the head, probably the brainstem, would be the weak link. Little did he know he would battle many more of the beasts in the years that followed.

Now, Adam bent down, grabbing this latest zombie's foot and dragging it toward the entrance of the cave. Then like a slow-moving soccer player, he used one of his own giant feet to pass the severed head along as well. At the cave entrance, Adam kicked the skull hard, sending it flying for several hundred feet out through the night and into the darkness of the forest.

Still holding the zombie's foot, he began to swing the corpse around and around, gaining velocity so he could fling the disgusting thing as far away as possible. During one of the rotations, the corpse took off, flying hundreds of yards out into the darkness. Adam realized the body had taken off before he had let go. He looked down and saw the thing's foot with exposed ankle bones jutting from tatters of moldering flesh still in his giant hand. He threw the foot as far away as possible with disgust and then wiped his hand on his pants.

His cave, the place Adam called home, was located high up on the side of a mountain hidden by countless pine trees. He hoped the stench accompanying the vile creatures would not be noticeable, but he had his doubts. He recalled a time not that long ago when the entire world stank of rotting flesh. Now the creatures were few and far between. These days, humans thought of them more as a nuisance than a threat.

He sniffed the air and could smell burning wood, not the scent of a nearby campfire but something much more intense. He looked out into the distance to where he knew a good-sized town stood many miles away. He could see the orange glow of a fire burning out of control.

"I can't believe they are at it again," he thought. "When will these people ever learn?"

Even now, after surviving a plague that practically wiped out humanity, these humans still felt the need to be at war. It was like people could only be satisfied if they were killing. And it didn't matter if they were killing zombies or one another. He recalled several years after the initial outbreak when the then newly reformed federal government began offering the general public the opportunity to collect bounty money by killing zombies. Although the program had an official name, people began referring to it as a Dead Kill bounty; the idea being that you were killing something, which was already dead. Survivors suddenly realized instead of running and hiding from these deadly monsters, they could earn a decent living by killing them. That was the beginning of the end for the undead. Soon what was once an ocean of roaming undead became a river, then a stream, and finally just a trickle, a fraction of what they had once been.

More than ten years since the dreaded Zombie Virus of 2043, also known as the Z43 Virus, started the zombie apocalypse. Yet now, years after the so-called zombie wars, humanity was still killing his fellow man, even though the act of doing so created more living dead. The Z43 virus still existed inside every living human, remaining dormant until the time of death when it activated. Years earlier, the government created preventive measures to dispose of any new deceased properly. These measures prevented the dead from returning. But in the case of war, there was no guarantee all the dead could be accounted for and would remain deceased. There was an excellent chance whatever skirmish had just occurred in that city miles away would create new monsters rising from the ashes.

It troubled Adam how humans still seemed to have this need to kill each other. From his observations, there were two facets of human survivors: the so-called civilized people who lived safely behind the walls of fortified cities and those called outlanders who lived like lawless savages in the wilderness outside the cities. The outlanders had turned their backs on civilized society in favor of a life free of legal restraints. The outlanders set up their cultures like tribes, with the most potent members leading the groups. Without laws to control their behavior for more than a decade, these survivors lived like savages, not unlike those not seen since the dawn of man. Most had even abandoned formal language, replacing it with monosyllabic gibberish nearly unintelligible. Not only were these outlanders at constant war with the humans inside the cities, but rival tribes constantly fought among themselves.

Adam wondered with a heavy heart just how many humans of both factions might have died in this latest conflict. The world had become a much different place than the one he had once known. So much had changed since his birth in 1792, or perhaps re-birth would be a better description. It was a hard fact to comprehend now in 2055, more than two and a half centuries later.

Adam didn't know if he carried the Z43 virus. True he was a man, but not a man like other men. He was not only different but unique. Perhaps this made him immune to the virus. It seemed to make him uninteresting to the dead ones, so maybe that idea might be accurate. Or it might be the circumstances of his creation that caused the walking corpses to leave him alone. He wasn't sure, but he hoped someday to find an answer. He suddenly heard groaning noises coming from the forest far off to his right. He realized more of the undead creatures must have followed the first.

His night vision was exceptional, and the bright moon further helped him see them coming. There were ten or more of the zombies in this cluster. If he simply stood still, Adam knew they would ignore him and walk by, but that would never do. They might find their way into his cave and fill it with their revolting stink. His shelter was not much, but it was his home and had been for decades. He could not allow these things to defile his domicile.

Adam charged headlong into the mass of rotting walking corpses using arms, legs, hands, and feet to dismantle the creatures. In a mad frenzy of savage destruction, Adam cut his way through the crowd, leaving not one of them standing.

One of the creatures had shuffled toward Adam, appearing to try to pass through him like he wasn't there. Adam slammed his massive hands against both sides of the zombie's head in a thunderous clap, sending brains exploding out of the creature's squashed mouth and eye sockets, like someone stomping on an open tube of toothpaste.

Two others were staggering about aimlessly. Adam raced at them, driving his fist through the face of the first monster and out the back of the creature's head. He pulled his muscular arm back, and the head separated from the thing's body but remained stuck on his hand. Adam slammed the decapitated head into the skull of the other zombie, succeeding in breaking that creature's neck and cracking open the zombie skull attached to his massive hand.

Two more zombies stumbled into view, one male and the other female. Adam walked up to them, palming their heads like an NBA all-star. He lifted them both up by their skulls more than two feet off the ground as they squirmed and struggled to get free. Then he began to close his hands, squeezing ever tighter. Within seconds their skulls crushed inward, sending shards of broken bones deep into their decomposing brains. Puss and grey matter oozed onto Adam's fingers.

After finishing the remainder of the herd in a fashion equally repulsive, Adam decided it was time to clean up. He tossed the remains into the woods to join those of the others. This cleanup was a challenging task not only because of the number of creatures Adam had slaughtered but because of the savage way he had dismembered them. He expected such carnage after he found himself in the throes of a rampage. The forest floor looked like a charnel house.

Adam stood for a moment, smelling the disgusting stench of the beasts. He looked down at his hands and clothing finding them covered in blood, puss, and bits of flesh from his savage onslaught. Adam needed to get clean. Walking along a path he knew well, Adam made his way through the woods to a lake where he stripped naked a waded into the shallows to rinse both himself and his clothing. His flesh, a patchwork of thousands of scars connecting flesh of varying hues, seemed iridescent in the moonlight. He examined himself for injuries but found none.

Seeing himself bared to the world made Adam think about his past and his life. He recalled as he often did about the man he thought of as his father. That man had been a scientist. No, he had been much more than a scientist; he had been a creator, a genius, and in Adam's opinion, a god. Yet, he had also been a cold-hearted, unfeeling man who had rejected Adam and hated him. Adam found it more than ironic that he should possess a kinder heart and more respect for humanity than the man responsible for giving him life.

He wondered not for the first time, what exactly was humanity? What is a man? Was he, himself not a man? Indeed, he must be as he was made from man. His father and creator had seen to that. And was he, Adam, not a good man? He considered himself an intellectual, perhaps not at the level of genius his father had attained. Still, he was knowledgeable and possessed a love for art, science, mathematics, music, and literature.

He was generally kind to his fellow man. Yes, he had killed in the past, both zombies and living humans as well. Early on, his killing had been out of frustration, rage, ignorance, and misunderstanding. Later he learned to control his impulses and kill only in self-defense.

His father had not thought of him as intelligent, just the opposite. He had even refused to give Adam a name, referring to him instead as "the monster," "the wretch," "the ogre," and other such derogatory terms. And when news of his existence became public, the townspeople had called him "an abomination," "a devil," and "a thing." They had tried unsuccessfully to destroy him on more than one occasion.

But in his heart, he believed he was a man. No, he knew he was a man, despite what others said to the contrary. Yes, perhaps he was a different sort of man, unique compared to any that had come before him, but still a man. He felt his father had slighted him greatly, and as such, he had chosen to give himself a name.

He recalled the day his father had been screaming obscenities at him and referring to him as something which the bowels of hell spit upon the earth. In one of his first fits of anger, Adam had risen in defiance and had shouted at his father, "I ought to be thy Adam!"

He decided right then to take the name Adam. And in further rebellion against his heartless father Victor, he chose to use his father's surname. He proclaimed himself Adam Frankenstein. He hoped that single act would do more to frustrate his creator than any other torture he might have imagined. And he was correct. Since then, the story of his creation had gained legendary status; most people now referred to him simply as Frankenstein. Despite his life of solitude, his knowing this fact seemed to make it all worthwhile somehow. His father had died in disgrace, and the world that had shunned Adam was now essentially dead as well.

Since the time he had last escaped persecution, he had led a life of isolation, knowing how people would react to the sight of him. If his height and massive size were not enough to instill terror, his thousands of scars from where his doctor/father had stitched together body parts were enough to horrify even the most tattooed and pierced of humans. Through the centuries, people around the world had claimed to see him lurking in the shadows. However, anyone who had the misfortune of actually meeting him face to face would take that knowledge to the grave with them. Adam was not happy about killing humans, but on occasion, it was something he had to do and which he had reluctantly accepted.

Even in 2053, in a world ravaged by a zombie apocalypse where rotting remnants of humanity still feasted on the flesh of the living, he knew he would be considered a horrible monster. He read rumors stating that the Z43 virus was mutating in living outlander humans during the past year. Rather than waiting until death to activate, the virus was causing living humans to mutate into an assortment of strange inhuman creatures, some of which supposedly were as big as he was.

Perhaps in another few decades, things would change. Maybe the virus would continue to mutate, creating a new race of creatures so disturbing in appearance that Adam would not seem so frightening. Until then, he had his cave, his literature, and an unquenchable thirst for knowledge to keep him occupied.

PARALLELISM

"Imagination is the parallel universe of a writer. If he is not
responding to you in the world, he is probably responding to
someone in the imaginary world."
—Heenashree Khandelwal

"I feel like I am diagonally parked in a parallel universe."
—Unknown

/ 1 /

The ceiling fan turned slowly above his head as Emmet stood watching, patiently waiting for it to stop. He had turned off the wall switch
a few moments earlier and what momentum remained in the fan was
strictly the result of its previous circular motion slowly winding down.
If he had been able to reach up and grab one of the five blades, it would
have stopped as there was no longer any power in its drive motor. But
it was too far away to reach from the bedroom floor.

The fan wasn't inaccessible high up on a vaulted ceiling or anything of that nature. It was located directly over his and his wife's
queen-size bed, which made it unreachable from anywhere around the
bed. Emmett had volunteered to help his wife Carla this weekend, and

he had just finished dusting the entire bedroom, save for the wooden blades of their ceiling fan.

He had once considered buying one of those fancy ceiling fan dusting thingies with a big fluffy oval brush on the end of a long telescopic handle, but their fan blades were only about seven feet off the ground. The problem wasn't so much height as location. Their bedroom wasn't large enough to move the bed around to get up at the blades using a stepstool. So, Emmett planned on doing what he had done many times before standing on the bed to reach the fan blades.

It wasn't the safest thing in the world, nor was it the most dangerous. Emmett suspected Carla had used a similar technique to dust the blades when it was her turn, though she might never admit it. And regardless of what method she happened to choose, if he were to fall and hurt himself, she would nevertheless chew him a new one. Besides, he had never had problems using this method previously. He may have had a few close calls at various times over the years, but no accidents. He wasn't getting any younger, sixty-five at his last birthday, and his balance wasn't quite what it used to be if he were frank with himself. As his late father used to say, "It ain't what it used ta was."

Emmett Parker was a part-time science fiction writer with several dozen novels and more than two hundred short stories to his credit. He had retired from his full-time engineer position six months earlier and supposed he could now call himself a full-time author. However, that title might be a bit grandiose since the little money he made from his publications scarcely supplemented his savings, meager pension, and social security income.

As he watched, the fan blade made its final revolution, and then it came to a complete stop. Emmett walked over to the bedroom doorway and listened to make sure Carla wasn't on her way upstairs. Then he went back to the night table and grabbed his dust cloth along with a can of spray cleaner. Emmett sat down on the bed and pulled up his legs as if turning in for the night. He took the rag in his left hand and sprayed it generously with the cleaner. Then using his right hand, he walked himself up the wall behind the headboard and soon was standing up on the bed, ready to begin his task.

He tried to be a quiet as possible so Carla wouldn't hear him floundering about on the mattress. He slowly approached the fan feeling like a kid in a bouncy house and appreciated why children enjoyed them so much. Emmett held onto one blade while dusting the others to maintain his balance. He felt he had mastered this technique over the years. Soon all five fan blades were clean of dust, and Emmett was ready to work his way down from the bed.

He started to back away from the fan blades. Suddenly an intense bout of vertigo overtook him. The uneven motion of the mattress likely brought on the sensation. He had experienced such a thing before, and it always passed quickly, but not this time. Before he realized it, Emmett was falling backward off the bed heading for the floor. He slammed his head against the wall and was knocked unconscious.

As he lay there on the floor somewhere between reality and unreality, he found his mind flooded with what seemed like thousands of scenarios representing what had just happened to him. Some were identical, some were slightly different, but many showed entirely different and often tragic results. In some scenarios, he saw himself almost fall but suddenly regain his balance then get down safely from the bed as he had done in the past. In others, he saw himself grab for the ceiling fan and pull it down with him in a shower of plaster dust. In yet others, he was lying on the ground with his arm broken in a twisted compound fracture, a bone jutting out from the skin. And in still others, he saw himself lying dead on the floor with his head cocked at an impossible angle, his neck broken. Over and over again, Emmett saw one different scenario after another played out, each ending differently and often tragically.

/ 2 /

"Emmett? Emmett Honey? Speak to me." Emmett could hear a familiar voice calling his name as he seemed to move in and out of consciousness. As he did, he continued to see more and more scenarios played out, so many that for a moment, Emmett thought he might go insane just trying to follow them all. There were thousands of images, all streaming like high-speed videos through his mind.

He heard a voice say, "Please stand back, Ma'am. We'll take it from here." Then a moment later, he was awakened to the spicy scent of ammonia in his nose.

"What? What the Hell?" Emmett mumbled, still disoriented, "What's going on around here?"

"It's ok, Mr. Parker," the voice said, "You just had a nasty fall and hit your head. You were out for a while, but you're going to be ok now."

When Emmett's eyes came into focus, he saw the face of two young Emergency Medical Technicians, one male and one female, who both were taking care of him. Behind them, he saw Carla standing watching with a look of utter terror on her face. He knew sooner or later there was going to be hell to pay for this stunt, but for now, it looked like he might be able to ride the pity train for at least a bit longer.

"Carla? Sweetie? What, what's going on?" He said in the most pathetic voice he could muster. After all, his head did hurt like crazy, and EMTs were treating him.

"You fell Emmett and hit your head," Carla said still sympathetically, "Don't talk. Just do what the nice boy and girl tell you to do. The two EMTs, who were probably in their thirties, just looked at each other. To Carla, everyone under forty was either a boy or a girl.

"Mr. Parker?" The male EMT asked, "Do you remember what happened to you? Do you know why you fell and hit your head?"

Emmett wasn't about to admit to having stood up on the bed to clean the fan, so he simply said, "I don't know for sure. I was standing by the side of the bed and must have turned too quickly, lost my balance, and fell."

"From downstairs, it sounded like someone dropped a bomb on the house!" Carla interjected, looking knowingly at her husband and not buying the story he was selling. She could see the dust cloth on the floor and the lack of dust on the ceiling fan. There were also visible indentations on the bedspread from his feet. She didn't have to say a word for Emmett to know that she knew. It was part of that unspoken language passed between partners who have been together for so many years.

"Well, here's what we're going to have to do, sir," The female EMT interjected. "We're going to take you to the hospital, and we'll have them do an MRI on your head just to make sure there's no internal bleeding or other such injuries. Plus, they might find out why you lost your equilibrium and fell."

Emmett argued, "I don't want to go to any damned hospital. Look at me. I'm fine. Just give me a few pain pills, and after a good night's sleep, I'll be as good as new."

"Don't you dare pretend to tell these fine people how to do their jobs, Emmett Stephen Parker!" Carla scolded, and Emmett went silent, suddenly realizing by using his full name that Carla had passed out of the pity stage and now was loaded for bear.

"Fine," Emmett reluctantly conceded, "But I'm telling you there's nothing wrong with me that a shot or two of whiskey and a good night's sleep won't fix."

The two EMTs looked at each other again as the girl rolled her eyes at the comment.

/ 3 /

As it turned out, Emmett had been quite lucky. He didn't have any damage to his brain, and even the threat of concussion was minimal. As a result, he was sent home after many grueling hours of tests and more tests, waiting and more waiting at the hospital.

Carla was by his side the entire time and didn't mention his accident or question how it had happened. As he waited to be released, Emmett had a strange feeling that he had experienced something unusual while unconscious, but he couldn't recall what it had been. Yet, the sensation wouldn't go away.

Carla drove the car on their way home, as the doctor had recommended Emmett have bed rest and no driving for several days. She looked over and said, "How are you feeling, Emmett?"

"I'm fine, Babe," he said, "Just a little bit off. I still have a bit of a headache, and my thoughts are a bit foggy."

She said, "Too bad. I was hoping you'd remember being up on the bed, dusting the fan before you fell."

"I . . . I . . . ," he stammered.

"Relax, Emmett. I could tell what happened as soon as I heard you fall. Seeing the clean fan blades and your foot impressions on the bed just confirmed it for me."

Emmett asked, "So you're not mad at me?"

"Oh yes, I most certainly am. I'm mad because I could have lost you today. Mad because you know better than to do something so stupid. But I'll get over it now that you're ok. It's just that it scared me so much." There was a catch in her voice.

"Ah, Jeeze Carla, I'm sorry. I'll try to be more careful."

"No, Emmett, you won't. And that's the problem. It's just the way you are. And I've to come to terms with the fact that one of these days you're going to do something really stupid and I'm going to lose you. And I don't know what I'll do when that happens. I don't know if I'm strong enough to go through something like that again." Her voice had a tremor, and Emmett realized she was fighting back the tears. He knew why.

He could think of nothing to reply in his defense. He understood to what event Carla was speaking. They had both survived that unspeakable event together twenty-five years ago and had moved on as best as they could. For a while, it looked like they might not make it, but they had found a way. Since that time, they often spoke of Stevie but never about what had happened. It was just too painful. They both knew it was not the best way to deal with things, but it was their way. Now Emmett was sure they were both reliving the tragedy. And it was his fault for being such a klutz.

But the truth was, Emmett was careless and tended to be accident-prone. Carla was right about that. But still, he had never come so close to seriously injuring himself or perhaps dying before. Maybe it was time he accepted his age and stopped taking such risks. A psychiatrist might suggest Emmett was unconsciously punishing himself. But for what? He had known tragedy; they both had shared one of the worst. But it wasn't his fault. Why would he punish himself? Then Emmett noticed Carla was turning onto Oak Street rather than continuing on Main Street.

"You're taking Oak Street?" He was going to ask why but realized it was irrelevant. Either road would get them home. It would probably be better not to question her since he was already in hot water.

"Yeah," she sighed, "I don't know. I just thought I'd try a different route home today."

He looked out the front window just in time to see a car speeding into the intersection from his right, ignoring the red light. He shouted "Carla" at the exact time she slammed on the brakes.

Tires squealed as their car slid into the intersection. Fortunately, the other car was faster, and their vehicle just missed crashing into the rear of the speeder as he passed by. When they came to a stop at the far side of the intersection, Carla saw the offending car zooming away, apparently oblivious to the potential disaster it nearly caused.

Carla sat trembling for a second as she cried, "Emmett, are you all right?"

But Emmett didn't reply. He sat staring out into space, appearing to look at nothing. But what Emmet saw in his mind's eye was a far cry from nothing. He was watching thousands, perhaps hundreds of thousands of scenarios simultaneously played out in his mind. Their car collided with the other in some versions, and both he and Carla were severely injured. In others, death claimed one or both of them. In some versions, the car missed them but collided with another vehicle or into a building, bursting into flames. In still others, they hadn't turned onto Oak Street, so they were nowhere near the accident. So many scenarios flashed through his mind in a few seconds that Emmett could scarcely comprehend them all.

"Emmett?" she shouted.

Emmett turned as if awakening from a dream and stared at Carla. His unknowing look frightened her to her very core. "Emmett, are you all right? Were you hurt?"

Still in a daze, Emmett said in a strange, detached voice, "I was killed. We both were killed. Then we weren't. We were safe. Then we weren't. Thousands and thousands of times over. Again and again."

"Honey, what are you saying? You're not making sense?"

As suddenly as the strange trance had passed over the man, it began to disappear. Emmett's eyes became clear and focused. He said, "I'm ok now. Yes, I'm fine."

"Are you sure, Emmett? You were talking strangely. Maybe we should go back to the hospital. Maybe they need to check you out better."

Slowly Emmett replied, "No. Honestly, Honey, I'm fine. Let's just go home now."

/ 4 /

For the remainder of the trip, Carla noticed Emmett sat quietly in his seat, appearing to be contemplating something, which he had chosen not to share with her for whatever reason. When they got in the front door, Carla helped Emmett to the sofa then sat next to him, placing her hand gently on his leg.

"Emmett. Tell me what happened back there. It was like you went away for a time or something. It was frightening."

After a moment, Emmett slowly raised his head and met his wife's eyes, and said, "I suppose in a way, I did go away. I saw things. Many, many things."

"You saw things? What kind of things?"

"I saw the accident, our near accident, played out in my mind with thousands of different endings, maybe millions," Emmett replied. "Some of the results we're the same as ours most were different, more catastrophic . . . and some were even fatal."

At first, Carla didn't know what to say. Her voice caught in her throat with a gasp. She had been in the same situation as Emmett, but she hadn't experienced such a revelation. Then again, she hadn't just suffered severe head trauma.

"Maybe it was just because the accident was such a close call. You know, maybe coming on the heels of your fall. I'm sure you're very susceptible to such things at this stage."

Emmett asked, "When we almost hit that car, did anything like that happen to you?"

"No, but to be honest, I think I did pee my pants a little. I'm going to right upstairs to clean up and get changed."

"I suppose I got off lucky then," he chuckled. "I also just recalled something else. I had a similar experience after my fall when I was regaining consciousness. I had forgotten about it until now. I saw my accident played out in many thousands of different ways. In some, I didn't fall. In others, I did and broke bones or was unconscious. And in others, I died."

Carla was stunned. What was Emmett talking about? Had the doctors missed something? Was his injury worse than they had diagnosed?

"Oh my God, Emmett. Maybe we should go back to the hospital," She suggested urgently.

"No. I don't think we need to, Honey. I'm feeling fine now. I think you we're right. I think the stress of the day may have been too much for me. You know I have an overactive imagination. Maybe the stress of the accidents just triggered something and put my brain into high gear. Let's wait a bit. I think if I just rest for a time, everything will be fine."

"Well, I suppose if you say so," She relented.

However, unknown to his wife, Emmett had an extreme suspicion of what had happened to him. He didn't understand why or how it had happened, but his science fiction writer's mind understood what it was he was seeing. He needed time to rest and to contemplate.

"I'm going to sit and watch TV for a bit and maybe nap," Emmett said, "The doctors did clear me to sleep, right? I know sometimes they frown on that when it comes to head injuries."

Carla assured, "Yes. They said it should be ok. I just have to keep my eye on you and check you from time to time. You're not feeling nauseous or anything, are you?"

"No, not at all. Just a bit exhausted from everything is all," Emmett said, getting comfortable and situated in his recliner.

"Alright then. Maybe you should just relax and rest for a bit like the doctor ordered."

"Very well, Nurse Carla. Say, maybe we should get you one of those sexy nurse's outfits. You know what I mean?" He wiggled his eyebrows, Groucho Marx style.

Carla did an eye roll and said, "Easy there, tiger. I think you've had enough excitement for one day."

/ 5 /

Emmett did sleep for several hours; however, it was anything but restful sleep. Images of alternate versions of his fall haunted his restless sleep—likewise, varying interpretations of their near miss on the way home from the hospital. The problem was the dreams seemed to be much more than just dreams. They appeared to be authentic, although alternate versions of the same reality.

He awoke with a start, still sitting on his recliner. He could feel cool dampness trickling down the center of his back. He lowered the recliner's footrest and attempted to stand only to realize his body was not happy with what he had done to it during his fall. He had been so focused on his head injury that he hadn't considered the effect on the rest of his body.

Every single muscle in his body seemed to be screaming with pain. His back and neck were a mass of knots, and his arms and legs felt like Charlie horses were just waiting in the wings to spasm when he least expected it. Even his fingers and toes ached. Emmett had been dealing with growing arthritis in those joints for the past several years, and his fall had done nothing to help relieve that discomfort.

He flopped back down onto his recliner, panting with a combination of pain, shock, and realization. Sweat streamed from every pore in his body. After a few minutes, he was about ready to make another attempt when Carla entered the room.

"I thought I heard you moving around down here. How are you doing?"

Not wanting her to know the extent of his pain, Emmett gritted his teeth and managed to push out the words, "I'm fine . . . just a bit stiff is all."

"I'm not at all surprised. That was quite a fall you had. I suspect it might be a long time before you'll try a stunt like that again. Are you sure you're ok, Emmett? You really seem to be sweating, and you look pale."

"Yeah, I'll be fine. I think I just need another of those pain pills the doctor gave us."

"I'll get you one right away," Carla said as she headed out of the room.

With his wife safely out of earshot, Emmett once again began what he knew would be the arduous task of trying to get out of the chair. After several agonizing minutes and lots of teeth-gritting as well as suppressed curses, Emmett found himself standing in front of his recliner, sweating, panting but still alive and able to move.

Carla met him with pills and water as he was leaving the room. "Here, Emmett. Take these; you'll feel better."

"I certainly hope so."

"Maybe you should sit down again for a while; you're white as a sheet."

"Honestly, Honey, I think sitting down is the last thing I need. All it does is stiffens me all up. I think what I need is a long hot shower. I would love a soak in a hot bath, but you'd probably have to call in a tow truck to get me out. So, a shower will have to do."

Carla looked at him reluctantly, then said, "I suppose that will be ok as long as you feel up to it. Are you sure you're all right?"

"Yes, I'm sure. I think this hot shower is exactly what I need."

"Well, then I'd better let you get to it then. Leave the bathroom door ajar, and I'll stop up and check on you periodically. Ok?"

"Of course. You're welcome to join me if you'd like," Emmett said, giving her his Groucho wiggling eyebrows again.

"Easy tiger. You're not ready for that level of exhaustion yet; hopefully soon, but not yet."

Emmett breathed a sigh of relief. The truth was that romance was the last thing he was ready to tackle. "Well, in that case, I'd better get my butt into the shower."

The shower was terrific as Emmett felt the hot water coursing over his aching body. If he were, to be honest, Emmett doubted if he had ever felt anything so good in life. Emmett wondered if the hot temperature was causing his heart to beat faster and pump his blood more quickly through his bloodstream. Since he just took a pain pill, he imagined the tiny particles of medicine racing through his veins like kids zooming down the tubes of a water slide. Just the idea of that seemed to make his pain subside. He assumed it might just be the placebo effect, but if so, then so be it. Whatever the reason, he was feeling much better.

As he stood under the refreshing water, his mind relaxed, and he could think more clearly. He recalled what he had seen. Emmett was more convinced than ever that he had somehow gained the ability to see beyond what he thought of as the everyday world. Perhaps it had been the result of his hitting his head and becoming unconscious. Something had caused him to be able to see into these other worlds.

He was an author of science fiction stories and was a fan of the genre as well. Although he had read dozens of stories about the concept of parallel universes, he had never given the idea any credence before; until now. And if he was right, and if he could find a way to focus this newfound sight beyond sight, he might be able to see someone Emmett never imagined he would ever see again. Even if just for a moment, it would be worth any price. If only he could see his Stevie again.

/ 6 /

Steven Ellis Parker was Emmett and Carla's only child. He had been a curious and intelligent little boy and had grown to be a wonderful young man. Carla had always hoped someday Stevie might attend one of the best colleges in the country. But unfortunately, that was never to be. In his junior year of high school, Stevie was walking home as he often did. It was the same route he had walked hundreds of times before without incident. However, neither Stevie nor his parents could know what fate would send their way on that day.

Harlan Edgewood was a local lifelong under-achiever who spent more of his time drinking than he did in any attempt to pursue a job. Harlan had mastered the art of working as little as possible and squeezing as much money from the federal government as He was able. He would deliberately take a job he knew wouldn't last very long. Then whenever it ended, Harlan would collect unemployment compensation. He'd ride out the unemployment as far as he could, occasionally doing odd jobs under-the-table for cash while still collecting from Uncle Sam. When his unemployment benefits were about to run out, Harlan would miraculously find another entry-level job and try to stretch it out until he was once again eligible for unemployment money. Also, whenever he managed to feign an on-the-job back injury, he'd do whatever he could to score himself some workmen's compensation money as well.

The fantastic thing about this was that Harlan could accomplish all of these things while being a raging alcoholic. Incredibly, he had never lost any job because of his drinking. He had been arrested a few times for driving under the influence nonetheless continued to operate his vehicle without the benefit of a license. Being a functioning drunk and cheater of the system were the two things in life Harlan had managed to do successfully. That was until one day when his luck ran out, and everything went tragically wrong.

Harlan had been driving down Elm Street one afternoon with a blood alcohol level far beyond what was considered legal. Driving in this condition was not new for Harlan, as this was pretty much how he went through life, whether behind the wheel or not. However, that day his reaction time had been significantly affected, much more than other times.

Young Stevie Parker was deep in thought, perhaps concerned about the upcoming SAT exams or thinking about a girl at school he was hoping to date. Maybe he was contemplating any one of a dozen other topics that occupy a teenage boy's mind. Whatever the reason, Stevie had stepped off the curb, and onto the street, at the exact moment Harlan Edgewood weaved drunkenly to the right and the rest, as they say, was tragic history.

Stevie had been struck so hard by Harlan's car he was knocked out of his shoes and thrown fifteen feet through the air before slamming into the trunk of an ancient oak, killing him instantly. Harlan slammed on his breaks, got out of his car, and staggered over to Stevie lay. The man sat down and began weeping uncontrollably, knowing whatever luck had carried him through life so far was gone for good. There was no way he could talk his way out of this terrible situation. When the police arrived, they found Harlan still sitting next to the body crying. Harlan was later booked and charged with vehicular manslaughter, driving under the influence, and a whole list of lesser offenses.

Harlan never made it to trial, having fallen into a significant depression over what he had done. Going a week without his much-needed alcohol did nothing to help alleviate his mood. It probably made things worse. One night Harlan managed to fashion a noose from his bed sheet and wrapped one end tightly around the bars in his cell door. He secured the noose end around his neck and forced himself down into a sitting position until the makeshift noose tightened sufficiently to do its job and take his life. Although Emmett and Carla were not in the least bit saddened by Harlan's demise, they knew it would never bring their Stevie back.

/ 7 /

Emmett finished his shower and got dressed in pajamas. After all, he had no intention of going anywhere else that evening as he was both mentally and physically exhausted. He called downstairs and told Carla he would lie down for a while in bed and maybe watch some television.

"Ok, Sweetie," she replied, "I'm going to finish up some things down here, then I'll be up as well. It's been a long day."

Emmett thought, "Incredibly long."

As he lay in bed with the television not yet turned on, there was a "what if" scenario going through Emmett Parker's mind. He thought again about what he had seen in his "visions." He supposed that was the right word for them, visions. He somehow had been granted the opportunity to look into thousands of what he thought of as alternate realities; parallel universes. In his mind, the concept was no longer some theoretical idea or an invention from the realm of science fiction. It did exist. Twice in one day, he had been allowed to see into parallel universes and to witness firsthand how things that happened in this world played out in other dimensions.

But what did that mean? Did it mean that every time something terrible happened to him in this universe, Emmett might see it played out in ways more devastating in other versions of the world? Would he someday learn to control this unique gift, that is, assuming it could be considered a gift? Would he eventually be able to see into other universes at will and learn what had happened to Stevie in those other places? Or since Stevie's death had occurred more than twenty-five years earlier, would it be too far in the past for him to see?

This idea made Emmett question the direction of his thinking. He recalled when he had witnessed his visions; Emmett had seen many scenarios where he had died. The day Stevie died, Emmett had never been called to the scene, even though it was only a few blocks from his home. As a result, his last memory of Stevie that day was of his being alive and well.

Emmett wondered if this "sight" would allow him to look back into the past to the day Stevie died. Then he questioned if he could even consider the possibility of watching his only child die over and over perhaps thousands of times only for the slim hope that he might see him survive in some of the other universes? If somehow it were possible for him to see his son alive and living out his life, would it be worth the price of seeing him not survive in others? Did he have what it took to do such a thing? Emmett doubted he did.

Then an image suddenly shot through Emmett's mind. It was a flashback to when he had fallen from the bed earlier that day. In one of the thousands of scenarios he had witnessed, he had seen himself lying dead on the floor with a broken neck, but instead of his wife, Carla standing over him, there was a man of about forty or so kneeling next to him crying. He hadn't realized it at the time, but now that he thought about it, that man looked very familiar.

"Oh my God," Emmett whispered, "Is it possible? Was that? Could that have Stevie?"

In whatever version of reality Emmett had seen, his son, his Stevie, had been there as an adult. Somehow Stevie had survived in that world. Perhaps Stevie he had decided not to walk home that day, or maybe that drunk, Harlan Edgewood had chosen to drive a different way. Possibly Edgewood didn't even exist in that particular world. It was also possible that Edgewood had died years earlier. The more Emmett thought about it, the more possibilities he could imagine. The number of scenarios was as vast as the number of parallel universes. The point was, in at least one universe, probably more, his son lived.

Emmett closed his eyes, concentrating, trying to remember more about that world and about seeing Stevie. Maybe if he tried hard enough, he could recall what Stevie had said to him. Had Stevie spoken? Or was this nothing more than the wild imaginings of an old man combined with the grief he still carried?

"Oh, Stevie," Emmett said as tears streamed down his cheeks. "I give anything just to know you were well."

Emmett heard a voice somewhere off in the distance calling to him. "Dad? Are you ok? Please, Dad, answer me."

It was the deep, baritone voice of a middle-aged man. Somehow Emmett knew that voice. It was like a voice he hadn't heard in more than twenty-five years, only more profound and more mature sounding. Emmett realized that was Stevie's voice, and he was nearby. But how could that possibly be?

/ 8 /

Emmett slowly opened his eyes, confused. Above him was the face he recognized immediately despite the advanced age of the man. Emmett said, "Stevie? Is that you, Stevie?"

"Yes, of course, it's me, Dad. Are you alright?"

"I . . . I . . . don't know. I think so." Emmett realized he was no longer on his bed but was once again on the bedroom floor. "Stevie? I . . . I don't understand. How can you be here?"

"I live here, Dad, with you. Don't you remember? I was downstairs and heard a bang. I came up and saw you lying unconscious on the floor. I called 911. The paramedics should be here soon. We'll have to have you checked out."

"But you can't be here, Stevie? I can't be here with you. It doesn't make any sense."

"It's ok, Dad. You're probably just a little confused. You bumped your head hard by the sound of it."

"Stevie. Would you please do me a favor? Go and get your mother. She needs to know what happened to me."

Stevie was silent, not sure what to say next. Then the front door-bell rang.

"You stay here, Dad. I have to let the paramedics in downstairs. I'll be right back."

"Don't leave me, Stevie. I can't bear to lose you again."

"Dad, don't worry. You won't lose me. You've never lost me. I've been here. I'll always be here."

A few moments later, Stevie returned with two young Emergency Medical Technicians, one male and one female. Strangely, although Emmett didn't know either of them, he felt as though he had seen them before. He recalled Carla's voice calling them a boy and a girl. To Carla, everyone under forty was either a boy or a girl. This was getting more confusing by the minute.

"Mr. Parker," the male EMT asked, "Do you remember what happened to you? Do you know why you fell and hit your head?"

A feeling of extreme déjà vu flooded through Emmett's mind. Hadn't he just experienced this same situation earlier that day, with the same EMTs?

The female EMT asked Stevie, "Has he seemed disoriented in any way since his fall?"

"Well," Stevie said reluctantly, "He's been a bit confused. He's been asking for my mother." The EMTs waited for further explanation.

"My mother died back when I was about sixteen. I was walking home from school, and Mom walked to meet me. She was hit and killed by a drunk driver."

Emmett heard a voice screaming, "Noooo!" He realized it was his own voice.

/ 9 /

Carla walked into the bedroom, ready for a good night's sleep after the trying day they had both experienced that day. She noticed the television was off and Emmett was sound asleep. She went into the bathroom to complete her nightly ritual.

When she came out of the bathroom, she noticed Emmett hadn't shifted position, and he seemed to be lying exceptionally still. She decided to shake him awake to make sure all was right. Emmett never awoke.

Days later, at the funeral, she took what consolation she could from the many well-wishers who all seemed to repeat the exact cliché phrase, "He's in a better place now. He's finally with Stevie again."